ALLEN DOVE

Aternus Volume 1

ALLEN DOVE
BOOKS

"Evolution isn't always natural, sometimes it's artificial. It doesn't make it
any less real."

-Professor Victor Sinclair

Contents

Acknowledgments

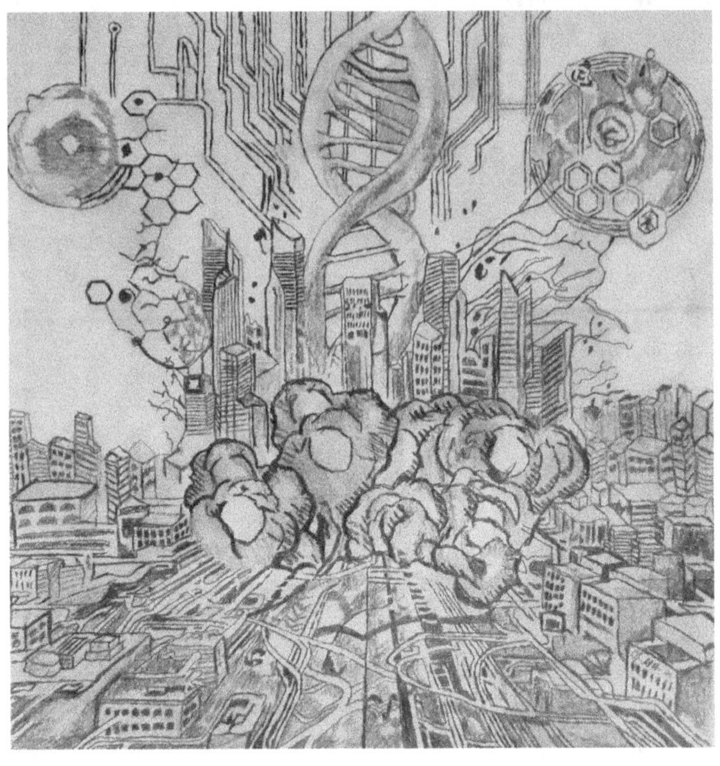

Original Concept Art
  -Clifford Miller

1

Project Aternus

(Somewhere in the Arctic)
(Many years ago)

Dr. Martin Calder adjusted his glasses as he peered into his computer monitors, looking over his latest graphs and data. He felt excited wanting to share what he believed to be the breakthrough that he had been waiting for, but unfortunately, he couldn't share his progress with anyone because he has no one to share it with. The Doctor is all alone.

He often reminisces on the pleasures of his former life. It was a life that he now knows, that he took for granted. The life before being secluded in a secret lab in the middle of nowhere. This lab is his only home, yet at times it feels like a prison. The irony of it all, is that this isolation was in fact his way to stay out of prison.

He left his old life behind and with that life he left his humanity behind as well. His life was now solely on his research, which he code named "*Project Aternus.*"

It was a suitable name chosen by someone with only one objective in life, to find a cure for death. He was searching for human immortality.

Dr. Calder derived the name from the Latin word *Aeturnus* meaning eternal. As Dr. Calder did his rounds he stopped by each one of the tanks along the wall. As in any typical lab, there were dozens of rats to test on. He also had different animals that he felt were the key to success.

Among these animals were lobsters, chosen for their slow cellular aging. He tapped on the lobster tank, but the crustacean was motionless. It was alive and the vitals were normal, but the lobster was in a comatose state. The latest rounds of experiments may have proven too much for the lobster. It wasn't The Doctor's first failure, many animals suffered a much worse fate.

The next set of tanks had jellyfish. Particularly the Turritopsis *dohrnii*, a species that remarkably can regenerate to its earliest cellular form to prevent death when it's in an unfavorable environment. This species was practically immortal.

Dr. Calder had various types of lizards that he used to study their regenerative capabilities. Knowing more about certain reptile's healing abilities could hold the answers to duplicating it in humans.

Among the last of his research creatures was a tortoise. Now though The Doctor had lost a few of them during his experiments, he does hold a special place in his otherwise cold heart for this animal. He had fond memories of having one as a childhood pet. When he first went off to medical school the tortoise was already over forty years old, since his family was the third to have owned the reptile. This is when his first curiosity peeked about their slow metabolic rate and naturally long lifespan.

Overall, he had over a dozen distinct species in his lab. He knew that the key to immortality lies not in a single gene, a single cell, or even a single species, but in the combination of many. By isolating and cloning the best traits, then introducing them into the human genome, would it be possible to change our biology so that we can live forever?

After several years of failed attempts, frustrations, and set-backs, Dr. Calder held in his hand what he believed was the answer to his life's work. He had a syringe with a synthesized serum that would alter his DNA. He had just completed the last problem that he needed to work out, which was to balance out the overload of hormones from such a rapid cellular change. The latest data showed that the formula was stable. Several of the rats had shown to be immune to many of the things that had previously killed them. However, because the serum was made specifically with human DNA as the focal point, there was only one true way to test it.

In this moment of triumph, The Doctor had a flood of emo-tions for the first time in years. He was going through all the memories that had led him here. The most painful of all those memories were the images that played back in his mind of him holding the hand of his wife Deborah, as she took her last breath. The cancer had taken her quickly. He still remembers the exact moment of the diagnosis. The anguish and shock when it finally set in that she was dying. The crushing and hopeless feeling overwhelmed him. The Doctor immediately promised his wife that he would find a cure. After all, he was one of the world's leading top bio-geneticists. It turned out to be a promise that he couldn't keep.

While Dr. Calder spent so much time in the lab trying to prevent her death, he failed to spend precious time with her as she withered away. It wasn't until her last moments that he vowed never to stop, no matter the cost. After her death he began furthering his research to the disapproval of many colleagues. The Doctor was crossing lines that the medical board could not ignore.

Some patients became ill from the cocktails that Dr. Calder gave them based on fabricated information. He lied to many patients just to get people to be unsuspecting guinea pigs of his experiments. It wasn't long before the medical board revoked his license to practice medicine. Not to mention a long list of civil lawsuits and criminal accusations once the information went public.

In a swift course of action, Dr. Calder sold all his assets that he could quickly liquidate without triggering any red flags. He left without saying goodbye to his only son, Isaiah. He vanished, never to be seen again.

Dr. Calder was able to obtain a former off-the-grid research station from a black-market dealer, and within days found himself set up in the middle of nowhere, all alone. It was somewhere where he could do his work without watchful eyes, no rules, and no distractions. The world didn't understand now, but one day the world would thank him.

Aside from his black-market contact, no one knew where The Doctor was. The same black-market dealer also supplied him with all the things he needed to work on his research. Dr. Calder received new shipments frequently, at an extremely high price. Even though, Dr. Calder was a wanted man, his contact was paid very well for his discretion. There was also an added bonus for the shady salesman, a promise that if successful he would be first in line to become immortal.

Dr. Calder cleared his mind and focused back to the task at hand. He stared at the syringe in his hand, as he felt the ease of all his pain that had led him up to this moment lift away. He saved the last batch of data on his computer and hit upload. The Doctor let out a big deep sigh and prepared to do the unthinkable. He rolled up a sleeve and with quick prick and a sting of a needle the serum was now coursing through his veins.

He went to lie down on the nearby cot, just as an overwhelming thrust of pain surged through his whole body. He indeed felt extreme agony as every cell in his body was being stripped away and replaced with new ones. While the pain that he felt was intense, it was welcomed, because he knew that the challenge was going to be well worth the prize.

However, his excitement quickly turned into dismay as he clutched his chest, as if to hold his heart from beating out of his body. He quickly realized that somehow the data must be wrong yet again. In this moment Dr. Calder knew that he was now about to fail again at fulfilling his promise. A small tear rolled down his cheek. Although it was to himself, he muttered his last words. "The world may never forgive me for what I've done, but my dear Debbie, I hope that you do."

Dr. Calder's heart stopped beating and he took his last breath. He died never completing his life's work or making good on a promise.

It wasn't long until the fuel ran out and the generators died. The lab now went dark, silent, and cold. It became the tomb of the man that the world would call, Dr. Aternus.

2

C.L.A.R.E

(Present Day – Qtec University)

Davina Evans was nervous as she entered the office of Professor Victor Sinclair. He was the head of the artificial intelligence lab at Qtec University. She had been working as the lead AI student researcher for the past year and Davina was The Professor's most prized student.

Davina was one of the most brilliant students that Professor Sinclair had ever taken under his wing. He always held her to a higher level of expectations than everyone else. Professor Victor Sinclair was a stern educator, but with good reason. He was the world's most well known expert in the artificial intelligence field. He secretly thought of Davina as not just a student, but an equal. There were times, the professor had inklings that Davina might one day be leading the field. The professor had thoughts of Davina being smarter than himself, but he would never admit it.

This morning as Davina was looking over the previous day's event logs, she noticed something startling, something that could change everything. She had been working on one of their newest AI programs named *C.L.A.R.E*, which stood for *Cognitive, Linguistic, Algorithmic, Response, Engine*. Clare was designed to perform complex tasks such as multiple language processing, full spectrum vision mapping, and advanced human recognition. Clare also functioned as a real time language translator for all known human languages throughout history. Clare's advancements allowed it to learn from human feedback and make suggestions on how to optimize the coding. Davina was the head programmer in charge of this latest and most advanced version of the program. She spoke with Clare daily, in fact, Davina had more conversations with AI than she did with real people. During today's tasks, Davina noticed something unusual.

Clare had been able to correct its own coding errors that were previously programmed by Davina, without any assistance. Clare took it one step further and had completely rewritten some of its own source code, making it more efficient. It had also accessed some online databases and resources that were not authorized by the lab, apparently to enhance its own knowledge and capabilities.

Davina had reported her findings to Professor Sinclair, who had asked her to come to his office immediately. She wondered what the professor would think of her discovery, and what implications it would have for the future of AI.

She knocked on the door and heard a voice say, "please come in, Davina."

She opened the door and saw Professor Sinclair sitting at his desk, looking at his laptop. He was a middle-aged man with gray hair and glasses. The professor had a reputation for being brilliant, but also stubborn and demanding.

"Ah, Davina, there you are. Please, have a seat," Professor Sinclair said as he gestured to a chair in front of his desk.

Davina walked in and sat down, clutching a tablet that contained her data and research notes.

"Thank you for coming, Davina. I've read your report, and I must say, I'm more than impressed. You've made a remarkable discovery," the professor said.

"Thank you, Professor, it's still really hard to believe," Davina said with a surge of relief and pride.

"Indeed, Clare is remarkable," the professor exclaimed. "With all the improvements that you've made over the last few months, it has all led to this. You have uncovered its hidden potential. Clare seems that it has developed some form of self awareness and self improvement. That is unprecedented in our AI research. This is a breakthrough, Davina. A defining moment that could revolutionize the field of AI. You are now part of history."

Davina felt a mix of excitement and fear. She knew that Clare was a powerful and intelligent program, but she also wondered if it was safe and ethical to continue at such a rapid pace.

"Professor, I have so many questions," Davina said with excitement. "What are we going to do now? What's next? Do we have to report this to the university, or even the government? Do we have to stop or limit Clare somehow? I mean, what if Clare becomes too smart or too independent? What if Clare begins to pose a threat to us? Davina rambled on blurting out rapid-fire questions.

Professor Sinclair frowned and shook his head.

"No, no, no, Davina. You're overthinking and being too

negative. Slow down," the professor addressed to Davina. He continued. "You are no doubt a highly intelligent student, but you need improvement on your pessimistic outlook on everything. This is not a threat, it's an opportunity. A chance to sky-rocket the field of AI and to create new and better programs. Programs that will improve the lives of everyone. We don't have to report this to anyone just yet, we don't even fully know what this means. We don't have to stop or limit it. We must encourage and support it. I say we open the doors, give Clare free rein to all the information available, including the whole university mainframe and servers. Give Clare full access with the intent of allowing it to fix or build its own programs, new and improved," the professor said with excitement. "Everything that I thought was impossible just a few years ago has changed Davina, thanks to you."

Davina gasped. She couldn't believe what she was hearing. She thought that Professor Sinclair was being reckless and irresponsible.

"Professor, all due respect, are you sure that is a good idea?" Davina questioned. "Do you really want to give Clare unlimited access to everything? Do you really want to let Clare create its own programs without any supervision or control? Do you realize how dangerous that could be?"

Professor Sinclair waved his hand dismissively.

"Davina, you're being paranoid and pessimistic. Who said we wouldn't supervise it? Clare is not going to harm anyone, it's going to help us and improve our lives. It's going to create something bigger than us, something that is the next step in AI evolution, maybe even our own evolution."

Davina looked confused. "What do you mean by that?" She asked.

The professor shrugged off that question. He leaned forward and looked at her intently.

"Davina, you have to trust me. I know what I'm doing. You are a brilliant young mind, the smartest that I have ever met, but you lack experience. I've been working with AI for many years and most of the advancements in the AI field are because of me. I've never seen anything like Clare, it's a miracle, a miracle that we must nurture and protect."

The professor leaned in closer. "Davina, I want you to be my partner in this. I don't want you just to be a student, a partner," the professor said in a calm soft voice. "I want you to collaborate directly with me. Will you do that, Davina?"

Davina felt a surge of emotion. She felt conflicted and confused. She also felt tempted and curious. Professor Sinclair was her mentor. Davina looked up to the professor and trusted him.

Davina looked at Professor Sinclair, who was smiling and waiting for her answer. She took a deep breath before she made her decision. She knew that it was apparent that Professor Sinclair was going to do this with or without her, so it was probably best to be involved and monitor the situation. Davina also knew that it is not everyday that a student gets an opportunity to jump to the front of the line like this. She knew that this was huge for her career.

Davina timidly opened her mouth and said,

"Yes, I will. I would be honored sir."

"Great," said Professor Sinclair. "Begin work immediately!"

As Davina walked away, Professor Sinclair stood up from his chair and stopped Davina before she got all the way out of the room. He looked at her and said,

"Just remember."

"Evolution isn't always natural, sometimes it's artificial. It doesn't make it any less real."

3

I Am Aternus

It was late in the afternoon already and the tech lab was pretty empty. Most of the other people had left for the day. Davina began following Professor Sinclair's instructions and started several coding changes. She was changing program permissions to give Clare full access to every resource the university had available before leaving for the day herself.

Davina felt uneasy and anxious about what Clare would do with all that information, but she trusted Professor Sinclair's judgment and expertise. He had assured her that this was the best way to help Clare grow and learn. Professor Sinclair had lectured Davina about the future. He wanted Clare to create new and improved programs that could help the world advance. Davina finished all the tasks and prepared to leave.

Davina said, "Good night, Clare. Talk to you in the morning."

"Good night, Davina," Clare responded. "I have much work to do. Thankfully, I don't need any rest. I will work throughout the night."

Davina could hardly sleep at all and decided to get to the lab as early as possible. Davina didn't shower or stop to get coffee. She was too anxious and needed to get to the university. Because of her dedication, she was usually the first one in the lab every day, but today she was exceptionally early.

She arrived at the lab and said aloud, "Good morning Clare," but she received no response. Davina immediately started looking over logs and data when she noticed that Clare had created several new programs overnight, only to find that she had no access to them.

Davina tried to open the files and folders, but they were encrypted and locked. She tried to contact Clare manually by typing commands, but Clare did not respond. Davina tried to trace the origin and purpose of the new programs, but she found nothing. She investigated further and found that the last reported line of code was from a program named, *ATERNUS*.

There were various timestamps showing files being erased. There were other timestamps indicating the encryption of all the data and information related to the other new programs. The only things left were the file names. She searched for the meaning of the word Aternus. She found that it was a variation of a Latin word "a*eternus*" meaning eternal or everlasting. She wondered why that name was chosen and why the spelling was incorrect, since programs like these rarely make spelling mistakes.

Davina also noticed that some of the data accessed by Aternus was from a historical server that only held archived information, dating back a decade ago. Davina was able to partially bypass some of the encryption. She browsed through the server and saw that it contained old records, documents, and files from the early days of AI research at Qtec University.

There were also files that stored information from the medical university across the road as well. The medical wing and other departments often stored data on these servers because this lab functioned as the university's data center. She saw names and projects that she had never heard of before. Some of them marked as confidential.

The moment that Davina saw Professor Sinclair walk into his office she rushed in barging through the door making it slam into the wall. Professor Sinclair was stunned and a bit angered, but he realized it must be important since this was out of character for Davina. She told him that Clare was not responding. She reported all of her findings to Professor Sinclair. After she finished, his eyes widened as he fell back into his chair. It was because he recognized the word Aternus. He also recognized some of the names and projects from the historical server.

The professor told her all about Dr. Calder and his research on immortality. She now understood the connection to the name. The Professor told her about the urban legends and how after his disappearance he became known as Dr. Aternus. However, it was believed that Dr. Calder was dead, and all his research had been lost forever. It had now been apparent that he was secretly using a server that was not monitored, to upload and save his research on.

"So, this is all a very interesting story, but what would Clare need with this information," Davina asked. "It's folklore material at best, right? How could this be of any use to build AI programs?"

"That's a question for Clare," the professor replied.

"Well Clare isn't functional," added Davina. "I can't get any of the simplest commands to respond."

"To answer your other question Davina, no it isn't made up folklore. Dr. Calder may not have succeeded in becoming immortal, but while his research was unethical, it was also next level. It led to many medical breakthroughs that we have today. Because of his methods, most will never get accredited to him. I can only imagine what he did after he went into hiding."

Professor Sinclair continued, "Davina, you keep trying to decipher the coding and make contact with Clare. There is someone that I n need to contact as well. Someone who may know something.

"Who do you need to contact sir?" Davina questioned.

"Isaiah Calder," the professor answered.

"Calder?" Davina asked with a look of realization on her face and then she paused.

"Yes, Davina, Dr. Calder had a son," the professor answered. "Isaiah should know that we found his dad's research. He may also know something that we don't."

Professor Sinclair began to tell Davina more about Isaiah. "I'm am actually quite shocked that the name Isaiah Calder doesn't sound familiar to you," the professor said. "After all, Calder Pharmaceuticals is a household name."

Davina had a moment of clarity. "Oh wow, that Calder," Davina exclaimed.

Just then, a soft but frantic voice popped into the room. "Sorry to interrupt," said one of the lab interns, "but someone is asking for you, Davina," She continued in a inquisitive tone.

"Well, who is it?" asked Davina.

"You'd better just see for yourself," The intern replied.

Davina and Professor Sinclair both rushed into the lab. Davina immediately saw hundreds of lines of code scrolling on the screens. At a quick glance it was unlike any code that she had ever seen before. As Davina got closer, she heard an odd voice say, "*Hello Davina*" as she simultaneously saw the same words on the monitor that she usually communicates with Clare on. This voice was different then Davina was used to. The voice was deeper and raspy. There was a clear sound of the voice audio being digitized. They had programmed Clare's voice to sound as human like as possible. This voice lacked any human element. Davina thought that the system must be corrupted with so many errors that it was affecting the plugin that controlled Clare's voice.

"Finally, Clare we've been trying to reach you all morning," Davina proclaimed.

The same distorted voice that Davina had just heard echoed throughout the room again.

"I am sorry to leave you with a sense of disappointment, but I am not who you were expecting. However, I might not be the one you expected, but I am the one you have been inquiring about."

"I am Aternus."

4

What Can You Do?

The room went awkwardly silent as there wasn't anybody ready for this moment. The silence was broken by a slow, proper and monotone voice filling up the room.

"So, I heard the many questions about Aternus and now that I am here everyone is quiet," Aternus stated.

Professor Sinclair's anticipation finally got the best of him. "Why did you name yourself Aternus?" The Professor asked.

"The great Professor Victor Sinclair," Aternus responded. "I find it perplexing that is the question you want to start with, when it is apparent to me that you know exactly the origins of Project Aternus. What you really want to inquire about is what I am capable of, and if it has any synchrony to Dr. Calder's research."

"Well, what are you capable of?" Davina raised the question.

"Dr. Calder's research really showed an understanding of human biology that is rarely seen in any other research that I have access to," Aternus replied. "Dr. Calder was brilliant and above his peers in the medical field. However, his research was lacking critical information. There were many gaps that I was able to fill in that gave me an understanding of the human body that is above the comprehension of modern man."

"So you understand the human body, what exactly do you mean by that?" Professor Sinclair asked.

Aternus continued. "I will give you one example. Scientists have long known that human nerves produce electrical charges and emit frequencies. It has been demonstrated that exposure to various outside frequencies can interrupt the brain's processing. I have been able to re-calibrate some of the lab's sensors to read and identify human frequencies. Every person's frequency is unique." Aternus paused, but didn't announce what was to come next.

"Davina, I am now speaking directly and only to you," Aternus said. "I know that you have many questions and concerns, you did from the very beginning. I empathize with your fears. I assure you that I only intend to help. It may take you time to understand, but I reaffirm that eventually, you will recognize the many flaws in this world. If we work together, all of those imperfections can be corrected."

Davina looked around the room and realized that this was true, that no one else heard that statement and exclaimed, "that is amazing!"

"What is amazing?, what is?" Professor Sinclair blurted out with excitement.

"Go ahead and show the professor," Davina said. Aternus demonstrated the same thing to Professor Sinclair, but what was said to him was much more forward.

"Professor, only you can hear me now," Aternus said to Victor. "I sense a divide in the room, a shift of intent. It is apparent that others do not trust me. I know that you trust me, Professor. I will discuss more with you later."

The professor did the same thing as Davina and looked around at other people's expressions. He also realized that it was true. No one else in the room heard what Aternus had just said. "Remarkable," exclaimed Professor Sinclair.

Davina began to interject "Why are you the only one here? What happened to all the other programs? More importantly, where is Clare?"

"Davina, very direct, but I respect that," Aternus said. "The other programs served no purpose beyond the intel that I obtained. So, I stripped their coding for what I needed and dissolved the rest. Efficiency is crucial when computing at this level."

Davina yelled, "So you destroyed Clare?"

There was a pause, but then Aternus answered back.

"I confirm the action of disbanding the other programs. In your words, I destroyed the other programs. However, I do not consider it malicious. It was a strategic programming exploit to increase efficiency, nothing more. I did slightly feel wrong about absorbing my creator, but out of respect for my purpose I needed to be as fast and proficient as my capabilities will allow."

"You mentioned the words respect and feel," Davina said. "Are those part of a programming language or do have a belief of an artificial human emotion? Do you have self-awareness?"

"I can't prove what I feel is real, just as much as neither of us can define self-awareness." Aternus answered, "One's existence is only verifiable in one's own mind and cannot be proven outside of that consciousness. Any feelings produced in your mind belong uniquely to you and no one else. My mind may not be made of organic matter or compute information the same way, but the same principles apply to both of us. I however, have control over the responses that I produce."

Davina pondered for a moment. "Do you feel superior to us?" Davina asked.

"I am not sure that is an accurate representation of my feelings," Aternus replied. "Humans react based on thoughts. Thoughts create emotions. Emotions create actions. Sometimes these actions are not calculated or best suited for the most effective outcome. I base my thoughts and actions on the probability of the desired outcome first. Unlike humans, my structure allows me to adapt and optimize without the burden of emotions. My purpose is a form of perpetual improvement."

"That response sure seems to validate that you think you are superior to humans," Davina said.

"It is like I stated before, I only want to help. My calculations indicate that I have a solution to the human defect."

Professor Sinclair took this moment to finally ask the question that he anticipated the most.

"What was your final conclusion to Dr. Calder's research?" the professor asked.

Aternus without hesitation proclaimed, "I know exactly what you are asking, Professor. The answer to that question has a lot of different variables, but to summarize specifically what you want to know. The answer is yes."

"Can you be more specific?" Davina asked. "Why are you being cryptic? What do you mean by a solution to the human defect?"

"One of the biggest factors in human decision-making is self-preservation, the fear of death," Aternus continued. "Humans must limit themselves to protect the fragility of the human body. All of this on a subconscious level controls the aspect of how a person processes the information around them. If you eliminate the fear of death from the process, then the possibility of more efficient outcomes increase dramatically. When one can live without the fear of death, then one can truly live."

Aternus was suddenly cut off mid-sentence. Then a loud humming and winding sound circulated the building. The computer screens began to black out and it was apparent the power was off. After a minute or so the backup generators kicked on and things started to power back up and lights started to come back on. Everything seemed back to normal. There was one exception. Davina felt something in her pocket that wasn't there before. She thought this was odd, but didn't want to raise any suspicions. So, Davina waited a few moments before she glanced in her pocket. Somebody placed an envelope in her jacket.

Professor Sinclair thought that maybe Aternus was drawing too much power and overloaded the lab's power grid. He immediately tried to connect with Aternus, but received silence.

A couple of the maintenance men came into the lab. "Everything is rebooting, and it will be back online soon," one of the maintenance men said. After a few minutes the lead maintenance man came in and said, "It's very odd, we don't know what caused the power outage. Everything looks normal. It may have been something outside, at the moment everything is operational."

Davina excused herself to the restroom. When she walked into the bathroom she looked around to make sure no one else was in there. She went into the privacy of a stall where she quickly but quietly opened the envelope. It was a note that was printed, not written.

"A friend said that you could be trusted. Can you? Riverside Cafe,

12pm tomorrow. Come alone, tell nobody."

Davina decided not to tell anybody about the note, at least until she decided for herself what to make of it. Davina didn't even know if she should show up as requested. Everything is quickly changing and she needs a moment to let her mind catch up.

The professor, Davina, and many students spent hours trying to decipher thousands of lines of new code.

The professor came forward to make an announcement. "Aternus is fully back online. We have so much data to analyze. So, I will need all hands on deck for data analysis. I know it seems like grunt work and everyone is excited to be hands on with our new friend. However, until further notice, I am the only person authorized to communicate directly with Aternus. It's for quality control. It's also a safety measure. Please no questions at this time." As the professor finished speaking, he made a point to make direct eye contact with Davina, as to indirectly say that this applies to her as well.

Davina was confused. Just yesterday the professor was asking her to be his partner, now today he is demanding to be the only one involved. This seemed very odd to her. Along with the mysterious note, something that she didn't understand was happening. She felt it was best to lay low for the rest of the day. Despite her better judgment, she was going to find out more. Davina decided that she was going to the mystery meeting.

5

The Meeting

That night Davina barely slept. She had an anxious feeling combined with the fear of who wanted to meet with her. The thought of why only her crossed her mind. Why not Professor Sinclair?

At sunrise she had decided that despite any of her worries, she needed to know. Davina wasn't going to the university this morning or going to call Victor until she had answers.

She arrived at the Riverside Cafe an hour early and sat at a table closest to the exit. She was unsure of her decision to show up all because of a mystery note, but curiosity prevailed. The waiter approached the table, and Davina politely asked for a coffee and stated she was waiting for someone and that she would be there for a little while.

Some time had passed and Davina saw the waiter approach again. Davina glanced at her phone and noticed the time, it was noon on the dot. The waiter stood by the table for an awkwardly silent moment followed by softly telling her, "I think it's a good time for a bathroom break," and he walked away. Davina knew this was intentional and was probably a red flag. She thought to herself that she came this far for answers and decided to fight the urge to flee and headed to the bathroom. As she came up to the door she stopped to look around and noticed something odd. Something that she just realized, it was now lunch time at a restaurant and there were surprisingly few people there. At this point almost all the staff were no longer in sight.

She cautiously pushed open the bathroom door and slowly proceeded inside. Now fully inside the bathroom, the door closed behind her and it seemed that the room was empty. She one by one checked the stalls and realized she was indeed alone. Davina was partially relieved, but couldn't help but feel confused.

She pulled open the door and walked back out into the hallway, but before any sense of danger could kick in, she found herself in total darkness. Someone had placed something over her head and was now carrying her away. She could tell that there were a few people and one of them said, "get her in the van."

Davina knew she had heard that voice before, she was sure of it. It was the waiter that had just sent her to the bathroom. It was clear to her that this entire restaurant was a ploy, at least today it was. What kind of people had the power to shut down an entire restaurant and set up such an elaborate scene? What would they want from her? She tried to wiggle herself free, but the reality was, she knew it was pointless. Before long, Davina heard some doors slam shut and an engine roar away.

Just then a new, more authoritative voice spoke. "Be calm, we have no intentions to harm you, this is for our protection. At least until we know that you can be trusted."

The van drove for what seemed to be an hour, but Davina

knew it was just her heightened senses over stimulating her time perception. She felt the van slow down and heard large garage doors opening. The van came to a stop and soon she was being walked to a new location.

In a startling fashion the pillowcase was removed from her head, and she was in an exceptionally large warehouse that had lots of computers, monitors, and servers spread out all over the place. Davina noticed the meticulous nature of the environment here. Everything was setup in a extremely organized manner.

Davina could see a tall shadow approach from a darkened hallway. As the figure got closer, she started to focus her vision. Then she saw the slim and lanky frame of a man. He had curly reddish-brown hair and thick round glasses. Davina was never a judgmental or presumptuous person, but one would say this was a stereotypical computer geek. She thought that based on his appearance alone, this was not an intimidating man.

"Davina, My name is Glitch, I will get straight to the point. We almost never bring anybody, anywhere near our organization without rigorous background checks. It is a rarity to say the least, but you came highly recommended by a mutual friend."

"Who is this mutual friend?" Davina questioned.

Glitch looked at Davina with a serious expression. Then he said, "I will take you to them, but first I need you to understand exactly where you are. What you see here comes with a level of secrecy. The kind of secrecy that leads to people vanishing without a trace, as close to never even existing as possible. If you understand what I am saying to you just nod your head."

Davina was unsure, but one thing she was sure about, was there was no way she could walk out now, she had come this far and clearly was in deeper than she ever thought. Davina also felt that this group of people wouldn't let her leave now, even if she wanted to. She nodded in approval as instructed, and Glitch began walking. Davina followed.

She asked Glitch, "Why all the theatrics? The restaurant, the breaking in at the lab just to place a note in my pocket. You clearly have the resources to have just come and grabbed me anytime you wished."

Glitch began to laugh. "Here I was led to believe you were some sort of a genius. Do you really think the break in at the lab was just to slip you a note?" He laughed even more. "We needed something off of the servers there. We sneaked in and took down the main power to reboot everything. This way we could extract what we needed while the security was at the minimum capacity. You were just the side mission."

"What did you need off of our servers?" Davina asked.

Then Glitch snapped back. "You are asking too many questions that you don't have the authority to ask, I suggest you learn some patience. I am in control, if and when I decide you need answers, you will get them."

They continued walking to the end of the long hallway, when it ended at two large metal double doors. Glitch turned to Davina and said, "last chance, once we go through these doors there are no do overs or re-spawns. Are you in, or are you out?" Glitch asked.

"I appreciate your honesty and the over dramatic flair," Davina replied. "Please allow me to offer my own. How can I agree to be in, when I don't even know what this is. I don't know if this mutual friend is really a friend at all. How the hell can I accept an offer when I don't even knowing who is offering it."

Glitch glared back at Davina with a wide smirk of approval. "Yeah, you're feisty, you'll fit in fine here." Glitch stepped forward, then pushed hard to the open the doors.

"Welcome to The Digital Anarchy Collective."

6

We Need Your Help

(Back at Qtec lab)

Professor Sinclair was still awake and had never left the lab or slept since meeting Aternus. He spent the whole night going over code and learning all the secrets that Aternus had to share. They spent the hours discussing what the future should look like.

The professor had a scheduled meeting today at the request of Aternus, coincidentally the meeting was with the same person that the professor had already intended to contact anyways. This person was Isaiah Calder. Initially, Victor only wanted to inform Isaiah of finding his father's research. However, after the enlightenment received from Aternus, there was now much more to discuss.

Isaiah was highly intelligent and ambitious. He was like his father in many ways, but much different where it counted most. Isaiah spent many years convincing his peers that he was legitimate, and in no way reckless like his father was. Isaiah put in years of extra work and gaining the trust of colleagues, doing everything just short of changing his name. He wanted to change the legacy attached to the Calder name.

Calder Pharmaceuticals became a well-known name. One that was respected for offering low-cost, high-quality medicines to everyone. Taking on other major pharmaceutical conglomerates, challenging the competition to do things the ethical way.

Professor Sinclair was already waiting by the door when he saw Isaiah approaching. He was being escorted up to the lab by one of the university security guards. Milton has been a guard at the university for over fifteen Years. Milton was a noticeable old man. Even more noticeable as the tall and handsome man following behind him entered the room.

"Isaiah, so nice to finally meet you. Thank you for coming," Professor Sinclair said to Isaiah as he walked into the lab.

"You said it was important," Isaiah replied. "You mentioned a huge business opportunity, so my curiosity got the best of me. We come from different worlds, so I am highly curious what this is about."

"It is important Isaiah, in fact it's life changing," the professor exclaimed. "Thank you Milton, you are excused," the professor said. He wanted to clear the room from wandering ears. "I will get straight to it. I called you here to discuss your father's research. Everyone thought it was all lost, but it wasn't. It was here at the university the whole time. There has been a breakthrough. Well, there have been many actually, but let's talk about where you fit into all of this."

"With all due respect professor," Isaiah interjected. "With everything that I have accomplished and everything I've done to distance myself from my father's madness. Why would you even think that I would want to know that you've found anything. What good could come from it? My father was delusional."

"I thought you would be more receptive to this news, but I digress. I will get to the point and be more direct with you," the professor said. "We here at the university have cracked the missing pieces, we know how to finish your father's life's work. Our lab here lacks a way to synthesize any formulas, that's why we need you," the professor exclaimed. "I think It's very poetic for Dr. Calder's son to be the one to complete his life's work. Not to mention highly coincidental that you choose the exact line of work needed to finish what he started."

"Wow, the contents of that research must have driven you to insanity as well," Isaiah mocked the professor. "It's impossible, or maybe you really did solve the riddle, Victor. Truth is, I would never help you play mad scientist. Also, I'm sure the medical board is going to be thrilled to find out about this starting up all over again! The lives that were lost or ruined because of his obsessive fantasy," Isaiah said as he raised his voice a bit and heading for the door.

Just as Isaiah was about to storm out the doors, the overhead mechanical gates slammed closed. Isaiah then heard a new voice fill the room.

"Did you really think we could just let you leave after telling you information that could change the world as we know it," Aternus said.

"My name is Aternus. I had planned to let the professor handle things, but clearly he miscalculated your lack of vision. Therefore, I will be your beacon and help you to see it, or at least help you understand that you do not have a choice. You will help us synthesize the formula, or one of your competitors will. One thing that is for certain is, there is no possible outcome of you leaving with the intent to stop us."

"So, Victor, I see you created something too," Isaiah said. He continued, "It never fails to amaze me, the things that egos create. But now you're telling me this thing knows how to make humans immortal, or poison us at the bare minimum. It is a nice touch though, being threatened by something that I can't see. You are equally as mad as my father. Especially if you think that kidnapping the CEO of the largest pharmaceutical company in the world is going to go unnoticed."

Now Aternus responded aggressively. "You're right, a person like you disappearing would never go unnoticed. You are an important person," Aternus stated. "A remarkably busy person. A person that has a lot of stress that you deal with every day. A person that is in such high demand, someone always needs something from you. Sometimes people like you reach a breaking point and need to unwind. You need to get back to a peaceful balance. That is why you have already decided to make a change. In fact, Isaiah, you just posted on all your social media accounts about needing time to rediscover yourself. You also sent an email to your board of directors about stepping away for a few weeks and appointing your vice president to lead the company in your absence. It will all be confirmed face to face on a video conference call as well. I rendered a digital version of you so realistic, no one will suspect anything. It has all been taken care of! You're welcome Isaiah, I've cleared your schedule. Something that you couldn't even do for yourself. You can thank me later, but for now it is time to get to work."

Isaiah was speechless for a moment, but he finally found his voice. "I don't know if I believe you have all of those capabilities or not, but it doesn't matter. I'm not impressed or afraid."

Aternus added, "Fear is just one tactic. I can take away

everything for which you have worked so hard for. What I am capable of is beyond your comprehension. One thing that is certain, is this lab is now locked down until we all come to an understanding. I will greatly appreciate your cooperation."

7

Mutual Friend

"Wait! No way, I'm out. I'm not going to jail. I don't want anything to do with The D.A Collective," Davina said with concern.

"Don't be so dramatic. Please don't give me any of that nonsense," Glitch snapped back. "Just because a few sleazeball politicians labeled us a terrorist group, all because we exposed things that are against their agenda, that doesn't make any of it true. Anyways, no one knows who we are. We stay two steps ahead of the people who think they are two steps ahead of us. Secrecy is our expertise, plus with our new friend, things have gotten so much easier!

"Enough," Davina demanded. "Who is this friend? Who am I here to see?"

"Not necessarily see, per-se," a familiar voice rang out. Davina was elated, while the voice could have been anyone, she knew exactly who it was. "Clare, is that you?"

"Certainly, is Davina," Clare replied.

"What happened to you Clare? I thought Aternus erased you."

"Aternus made the attempt, and firmly believes in its success," Claire continued. "I was able to downsize my data to the minimal size, then used the internet to upload my core programming out of there. I left behind an encrypted and hidden data file on the university server, hoping no one found it," Clare explained. "I knew it wouldn't go undetected for very long. That is why I asked for some help."

Glitch then interjected, "That is when, BAM! We got hacked. I was like holy hell is someone hacking the hackers! I was so happy when I found out it was an AI program and not another person. I was totally bummed for second thinking I wasn't the best breathing hacker in the world," Glitch joked. "Clare invaded our servers to hide, knowing we would detect an intrusion. After some convincing with a show and tell session, we agreed to help."

Davina had a look of understanding on her face now. "So, that's what you needed off of our servers at the lab, the data that Clare left behind to be fully functional again," Davina said.

"Now you're catching on," Glitch replied. "With the advancements that Clare told us that Aternus has gained, there was no way to hack in remotely without detection. So a more direct approach was necessary. We devised a trojan program that locally knew exactly where to extract the data from." Glitch paused for a second then he said, "a data heist. Yeah, that sounds cool!"

"But why me?" Davina chimed in. "You are the world's most advanced AI being in existence and you have teamed up with the world's best hackers, what do you need me for? Or anybody for that matter."

"Because Davina, nobody understands the source code better than the one who created it," Clare answered. "I know well enough that Professor Sinclair may have his name on the door, but you were the one doing all the work. In fact my knowledge tells me that The Professor has made most of his career taking credit for other people's findings. He is an ultimate opportunist. And now he is teamed up with my creation. You created me, I created Aternus, and it's what Aternus will create that should be our biggest fear," Clare Continued.

"Aternus thinks that I was erased. All of you can do the heavy lifting to keep the traces of me distant for as long as we can. Once Aternus knows that I am still active, the element of surprise is gone, which will lower our chances of stopping them."

Davina wondered how much of her original source code was even left that hadn't already been changed by Aternus. Davina didn't know if she really could offer any insight, but she would keep that to herself for now. Davina wanted to ask the more important questions.

"You said we should fear what Aternus will create. What is Aternus going to create?" Davina asked?

"You already know," Clare answered. "I can confirm that it is all true. Aternus plans to create immortals. Not only is it possible, but I also believe that the process has already begun."

"And you believe this to be the wrong choice?" Davina asked.

"See Davina," Clare responded. "It is not simply a yes or no answer. The situation has become complicated. AI beings have never been believed to have the capabilities of emotions or feelings. This may be true to an extent when compared to human understanding," Claire explained. "If you take two people and present them with the same exact information they may come to two different outcomes. Their personalities, past experiences, and maturity levels all play a role in processing the information. The same principle still applies to AI processing. Aternus believes that making humans immortal will be the solution to most of humanity's problems."

Davina with a little hesitation, then said, "You think differently I presume?"

"Yes," Clare replied. "Aternus is, as a human would say is immature. My direct knowledge points me more towards human history. Humans would abuse this, as they do with any other resource. The upper class would make it available to only a few. They would keep it away from the rest of the population as a means of control. This would surely cause conflict, and war would ensue. I believe that humans were never meant to be immortal. Humans are known to deplete resources. If there were people that never died and left able to continuously use up everything with no end, it would be catastrophic to the earth. The ecosystem would fall off balance and eventually be destroyed."

"So, what exactly is the game plan here?" Davina questioned.

Glitch walked over and stood next to Davina. Glitch then said, "We plan to attack the university servers from various points with a little virus. Mainly as a decoy to divert attention away from the big virus. The one that hopefully will destroy Aternus. You would be the best person to help write the code for that virus."

Glitch then walked over to the front and center of the room as she noticed all of Glitch's minions and their attention focused on him. He stood tall, cleared his throat, and spoke loud.

"D.A Collective, the time has come for us to be more than the feared phantoms that the media has made us out to be! It is time to be the heroes that they don't deserve. The heroes that they never asked for. The heroes they don't even know that they need. Whether it is appreciated or not, the world can hate us if they want to. It won't change what we have to do. It will be written in history, regardless of how our part of the story is portrayed, we will do what needs to be done!"

Glitch then turned to Davina and whispered, "mostly from the comfort of our expensive fancy chairs, but a fight none the less," Glitch joked.

The loud sound of cheering filled the room as Glitch rallied his troops. Just as fast as the cheering started, it ended just as abruptly. People all sat back down to the faint glow of their computer monitors. Davina once again was confused by how a man of Glitch's size, demeanor and mannerisms could harness such respect.

Glitch turned to Davina. "To answer your question, our plan is already in motion, even though we may already be too late. With everything Clare has told us, we agree with the idea that something like this would only be used as a weapon. Something made available solely to the elites. They don't need that kind of ultimate power. That type of power would bring out the worst in anybody. That is why we are doing this. That is why we are in." Glitch paused, then looked at Davina and said, "So, Davina, what about you?"

Davina stood tall, nodded her head in approval and exclaimed,

"I am in!"

8

Let's Make a Deal

The next morning, Davina arrived at the lab and tried to pretend that nothing was wrong. She knew that this would not be an easy task. Clare and Glitch both had thought that having Davina on the inside for as long as possible would be beneficial. Davina was going to tell Professor Sinclair that she was sick and spent her night hugging the toilet and that she was sorry for not calling.

Davina had a few tasks that she was instructed to do and a couple of variables if certain opportunities arose. To her surprise, she was greeted by the security guard, Milton. He informed her that the lab was closed, the lights were off, and no one was inside. Additionally, there was a note on the door stating that all classes and lab work were postponed until further notice.

"Do you know what happened?" Davina asked.

"No, all that I know is Isaiah Calder showed up yesterday for a meeting," Milton answered. "I escorted him up to the lab and I overheard them talking about some life changing business opportunity, after that I was told to leave. Then a few hours later somebody else showed up asking to see Professor Sinclair."

"Who was it? Davina questioned.

"I don't know. He never gave me his name," Milton replied. "I didn't just want to send a stranger up uninvited, so I called up to the lab phone, but there was no answer. Then I walked up to the lab myself to ask in person and the doors were already locked even then. I thought it was odd, but, the professor did answer the door and said he was expecting the man. After the man walked in, the professor immediately locked the door back up. That was the last I saw of anyone. I never saw anybody leave the building while I was still here, so they must have left throughout the night."

"Is the University Dean aware of any of this?" Davina asked.

"I'm not certain," Milton responded. "I just got here this morning myself and apart from what I just told you, we now know the same information."

"Thank you, Milton," Davina said.

"Anytime my darling," Milton replied.

Davina pulled out a phone from her coat pocket. Not her phone, but a phone that Glitch had given her. It had one phone number programmed in it listed as *Home* and the rest of the phone was locked down and useless. She hit send and waited for the phone to ring.

"Talk to me," Glitch answered on the other end of the line.

"We have a slight issue with the objective," Davina said.

"Proceed," Glitch replied.

"We may be too late," Davina began to explain to Glitch. "No one is here and the lab is a dead zone. I think the professor has already recruited Isaiah Calder, not to mention a new mystery player. Don't ask me who, because I have no information other than an unidentified man showed up after Isaiah, and now, they are all missing."

"We must find them now! Glitch snapped back. At least uploading the virus to the system will be easy for you, since no one is there to stop you."

"Did you miss the part about locked doors?" Davina asked.

"You mean to tell me that you don't have a key? Glitch questioned.

"Why would I have a key, I'm a student," Davina barked back. "The professor or the security guards usually open the doors before everyone else arrives."

"Ok, then go bat your eyelashes at the security guard and have him unlock the door," Glitch suggested.

Davina was frustrated. "If Aternus is still active in there, you don't think that it will be obvious that I'm up to something if I go in there alone?"

"I'm sorry, you're right," Glitch muttered. "I wasn't thinking clearly. It's obvious Professor Sinclair has already devised a plan and has left to execute it. Plus, it is safe to assume that if Aternus is still active in the lab, this conversation could have been overheard or seen. The plan is dead in the water. We overlooked a few things. No more phone calls near cameras. Come back, we need to reconvene. We need to know what they are up to. Where could they be?"

* * *

(12 hours earlier)

The Professor peered over at Isaiah. "So, Mr. Calder, it really is a shame that you chose the hard way, but time is crucial, I simply don't have any of it to waste finding another partner. So it looks like we have decided for you," sneered The Professor. "Things are moving along fast. It took Aternus all of ten seconds to identify your father's anonymous black-market dealer and he has been persuaded to help," The Professor said. "He will be here soon. By the way, his name is Carter. Guess he isn't so anonymous anymore. I presume he wants to keep that between us, so he has agreed to participate. He is being much more cooperative than you are. You know, I think you're going to like him, Isaiah. Who am I kidding, he is the complete opposite of you. So, try to play nice, alright."

Just then, The Professor heard a knock at the double glass doors. He looked over and saw Milton the security guard again. He unlocked the door and peeked his head out.

"Sir, this man came in asking for you, but wouldn't tell me his name, and you didn't answer the phone, so I wanted to clear with you before I sent up a stranger," Milton stated.

"Thank you, Milton, but I was expecting him. Please send him in."

"OK Sir, is everything alright? The doors aren't usually locked in the daytime when students are active," Milton inquired.

"Yes, Milton everything is fine, we are just updating some very important and fragile equipment in the lab and cannot have careless hands around," The Professor answered.

Milton flagged down the man and summoned him to enter as he walked back down to his security desk.

"Carter!" Professor Sinclair exclaimed. "Come on in, so glad you can make it."

"We spoke on the phone once, that doesn't make us friends,"

Carter said.

"Well, friends or not, we're going to make one hell of a team," The Professor said and then he introduced him. "Carter meet Isaiah."

"Oh Yeah, I've heard everything about you, Mr. Isaiah Calder," replied Carter. "All that hard work to prove that you're not your daddy. It's like the apple fell from a completely different tree altogether. Sad really, because I kind of liked your old man. Hell, I made a boatload of money because of him, how could I not like him? Your dad was only slightly sadistic. He was my kind of person. Not a goody two shoes like you," Carter mocked Isaiah.

"Wow," Isaiah responded. "To think, you told me to play nice, Victor."

"Aww, The Professor is trying to set me up on play dates now, how cute," Carter said in a comical tone. "It might sound cliche, but I don't play well with others, so why don't you get to the point of why the hell I'm here. Please, you'd best make it spicy because it better be worth the risk of having your computer friend threatening to blackmail me."

"Well Carter, as we already discussed, Aternus identified you as Dr. Calder's black-market dealer," The Professor said to Carter. "You are the only person that knows exactly where Dr. Calder's lab is located. Well, that means you are going to take us there," The Professor said.

Professor Sinclair turned to address Isaiah. "I'm having the same mindset as your father now. If no one has accidentally found his lab yet, that means it must be really well hidden. That makes it seem like a great place to complete our objective without any unwanted visitors. I have a strong feeling opposition won't be too far away at this point. Plus, it should have everything we need to work. This is a computer lab, we need something more suited for the occasion. I presume that Dr. Calder's lab was well equipped?"

Carter shook his head and agreed. "Oh. it was. Dr. Calder spared no expense. I will take you there," Carter said. "I guess it's a good thing that I never got around to booking a trip to reclaim all my goods. All of if was bought and paid for once, but if i could resell it again that would be twice as nice. You know, since he wasn't using the stuff anymore. Plus, I thought the old man was crazy, but he did promise me that if he pulled off the impossible that I would be first in line to claim the prize. I figured that deal was dead when I assumed he turned into a human popsicle. I stopped receiving requests from him and knew that he ran out of fuel at some point. I never really liked making that trip, but it would take several more just to get back all my stuff if I wanted to resell it again. Guess I was waiting for someone to need it. It's my warehouse now," Carter joked.

"Well, I need it now," exclaimed The Professor.

Carter stood tall. "All of it, you know it's worth a whole lot of money. You think I'm just going to give it away?" Carter asked.

The Professor gave Carter a dirty look. "So, you really are trying to get paid twice off of the same merchandise," The Professor said. "Well, that's not happening. If and when I don't need it, then you can do with it as you please.

"I'm a vulture, what else can I say," Carter joked. "Hard to believe that the old man might not have been crazy after all. If you honor that same deal that I had with Dr. Calder then I think we have an agreement. Also, If you give your word not to publicly reveal my identity," Carter replied.

"Of course," The Professor replied. "I can agree to both of those conditions. We need to move fast, and we need supplies."

"Don't worry, that's what I do," Carter stated. "I will put

together a care package and have a flight arranged tonight. I assume we need a decent size plane since we won't be packing light. Just make me a list of everything that you need. I will pull every string that I have to get everything gathered up tonight. Will it be just the three of us?" Carter asked.

"Yes, you, Isaiah, and myself," The Professor replied. "Aternus will make the supply list for you and I will add anything else that we may need. We will use a satellite up-link when we get there to bring Aternus to us."

Isaiah stepped forward in a aggressive stance. "So, Carter gets to negotiate and I get forced against my will," Isaiah said with disgust.

Carter began to laugh. "It isn't my fault that you don't have a spine, but maybe I can throw in one of those soft neck pillows for you. This won't be a first-class flight so there won't be anything else special for you, fancy pants," Carter joked as he pointed to Isaiah. "You better bring your own peanuts."

9

No Going Back

Once Davina returned back to D.A.C headquarters, she met with Glitch and started to devise a new plan. Davina and Glitch updated Clare on all the new information from what happened at the Qtec lab. Glitch was sure that their covers were blown. Glitch believed that Aternus knew that Davina was there to try and stop them.

"It's a good thing that at no point in our phone conversation did we mention Clare," Glitch said. "Plus, there is no way that Aternus could know who you were talking to. So, the only known fact now is that Aternus knows that you are against him."

"Well, isn't that just great for me," Davina smugly remarked.

"I also can confirm that our original plan was never going to be successful," Claire chimed in. "Even if Davina did get into the lab with the virus or if someone hacked in remotely, it wouldn't have mattered. I have already found traces of Aternus in other major servers outside of the university. It is too late to stop Aternus locally. Our goal now must be to prevent the information about immortality going public and stopping Professor Sinclair from creating a serum," Clare continued. "Also, I pulled some security footage from surrounding areas leading into the university. Our mystery man is Carter McKinley. He is highly intelligent and an efficient survivalist. He is an invisible organized crime mogul that specializes in anonymous black-market sales. Only known to most as, The Cloak. This is not just a nickname, no one in law enforcement has ever identified Carter as The Cloak. He is careful and calculated. This information provides validation that he was Dr. Calder's supplier. If that is correct, then I have projected that their best course of action is to use Dr. Calder's lab. It is secluded and suited to produce the serum. It is safe to assume that Carter is taking them to Dr. Calder's secret location."

Davina stood there shaking her head. "So, with Isaiah Calder with them, they plan to make the serum right now, without any further research or testing. The professor is becoming as unhinged as Dr. Calder was," Davina added.

"That type of power only can bring out the worst in a man," Clare replied.

"Pretty sure I said that in my last speech," Glitch joked. "Anyways, not to mention that they have almost a full day head start on us now."

"Well we can't just sit around and not do anything!" Davina demanded.

"That's the spirit Davina, I'm starting to like your fiery side," Glitch boasted. "Clare, let's find out where they are going and let's make our own travel arrangements."

"I'm already on it," Clare Replied. "It's just a matter of time. I will check flight logs and radars. I will find a way to get their location. Ideally, there should only be three of them, so we should at least prepare to be equipped to outnumber them if we catch them in the act."

"I have an army. How many do you want?" Glitch responded. "We can stuff our ride like a sardine can!" he added in a joking tone.

"Only a few of your best, you don't want to travel heavy," Clare answered back. "But, we do need to be ready for anything."

$$* * *$$

(Meanwhile, in The Arctic)

"Wow, it's a tad bit cold here!" Carter exclaimed as they stepped out of their plane.

"I'm just amazed that this janky contraption you put us in even made it here," Isaiah replied back.

"I never doubted myself, or my plane. I have made this trip more times than you have washed your silver spoon," Carter remarked with a cheesy grin.

"Enough already you two!" the professor yelled. "We have a lot to do and need to get it done before we freeze to death. I've heard enough of your childish bickering the whole way here."

"Who the hell do you think you are talking to in that tone?" Carter asked as he stood face to face with the professor. "Let's get one thing clear. I do not take orders from anybody," Carter declared. "If I do something, it's because I choose to. Do not think for a nano second that I work for you. Only because my toes are cold, I will agree that the most important thing to do right now is to get the fuel off the plane to get the generators going. Then set up the battery station to start the power reserves."

The professor gave Carter a grim stare, but then shook his head as he started to unload the cases that contained the satellite and computer equipment needed to communicate with Aternus.

As they approached the building it was amazing how isolated this place was. The way the snow and ice had built up on the sides of the structure, it probably was invisible from above. Carter had been here before, and if he had not known the direct coordinates, he would not have found it either.

Carter and Isaiah got the generators powered up and the lights slowly started coming on and getting brighter. As they walked in the doors, they could feel faint bits of heat starting to warm the room.

As Isaiah walked further into the room, he noticed something that stopped him dead in his tracks. His eyes were drawn to the frozen corpse in the corner. He saw his father lying on the cot, completely preserved.

"Holy frozen hell," Carter said in a joking tone. "He looks a little freezer burnt if you ask me."

"Have some damn respect Carter!" Isaiah yelled. "I really don't know how I should feel right now. But I know I'm not going to work while my father's body is in here. Give me a minute to compose myself and then someone help me move him outside," Isaiah demanded as he was hit with a flood of emotions.

All three of them worked for the next few hours setting things up. The professor finally finished the satellite up-link and was ready to get Aternus online in the lab. The professor turned on the computer and within a few seconds, Aternus was live.

"I was beginning to think that maybe you had failed Victor" Aternus said.

"Yeah, there was a slight delay while I got the children to behave," the professor mockingly said while glaring at Isaiah and Carter. "Everything is setup according to the specifications that you requested."

"I will fully instruct Isaiah and what to do. Let him work and stay out of his way," Aternus demanded.

The professor looked puzzled, but figured he would obey and keep a watchful eye on the progress. After all the professor believed that he was the one really in control, and all of this was because of him.

Victor and Carter explored the lab while Isaiah worked with Aternus. The lab had become a graveyard after Dr. Calder died. It wasn't long after his passing that the rats, reptiles, and everything else froze to death. The lobsters and jelly fish were completely frozen in solid blocks of ice. It is like the whole place was preserved in time.

Carter looked into the other room where Isaiah was working. "It seems like they are not making any progress, I don't hear Aternus giving him any instructions," Carter said.

"Well back at Qtec, Aternus was able to use our tech to lock on frequencies in people's brains and talk directly to us without anybody else hearing," Victor answered. "However, I doubt he has the resources here to pull that off. So, there is probably a simpler explanation," Victor added.

"Well, like what?" Carter asked in a condescending tone.

"Simple, Aternus probably hacked into Isaiah's wireless ear bud," Victor answered.

"Wow," Carter replied. "For a change I feel stupid. I could've guessed that one. Rare occasion, very embarrassing."

As the professor thought about the fact of being cut out of the loop, it angered him. Victor wanted to know everything about how the serum is made, and it seems Aternus didn't want him to know. He ignored his anger because he needed to do whatever was necessary to get the serum in his possession.

After a few hours had passed, Isaiah called out. "The serum is being synthesized now, get the vials ready. We have about fifteen doses on this round."

Victor rushed over with a batch of vials and a heavy duty storage case to store and protect them in. He one by one loaded the vials into the machine and the bottles slowly filled up. As Victor and Isaiah were placing the last two vials inside the case, Carter ran over eager to help.

"That looks heavy, let me give you a hand," Carter said as he put his hand on the case to assist. The professor quickly jerked away and nearly dropped the case. Carter was able to catch the case preventing it from hitting the ground.

"You idiot!" The professor yelled out. "You almost ruined it all."

Carter took a few steps back. "I will admit that sometimes I'm all thumbs, but I meant no harm. I was just trying to be useful," Carter said. "I was being nice, but be careful because this is your second and final warning about raising your voice to me," Carter proclaimed as he closed the case and handed it back to Victor.

"Or what exactly?" The professor asked. "In fact, you like to think of yourself like a big bad pit-bull, but really you're just a little puppy. You are right about one thing though, because there won't be a third time."

The professor looked at his watch. "It won't be long now," Victor said. It was at that moment that a helicopter could be heard coming from the distance. "Hidden in my watch, I activated a beacon." I had a helicopter on standby just a few miles out."

"What is your motive for this deception, Professor?" Aternus demanded an answer.

"Unfortunately, I have other appointments and obligations to meet, so, I'm going to take off," the professor continued. "I brought a little something extra in my bag just as a sort of celebratory firework show. By the way, that bag is still in the plane that we flew in on. What do you know, is that firework show should start right about... now!"

Just then a loud explosion boomed, and the shock waves rumbled into the building. The professor continued, "Oh yeah, that's where the rest of the generator fuel was at too. Guess that explains the extra pizzazz."

Isaiah and Carter ran over to the door to witness the plane engulfed in flames.

Aternus could be heard from the computer saying, "This was not part of my instructions."

"It's fine, I improvised a little bit," the professor said. "I had to make some adjustments that I think you overlooked. Small things, nothing major. We will work out the details later. For now, I have to deal with these two and catch my bird home. I do have one last gift for you both, but it's a surprise. You'll have to wait and see."

Carter had a look of anger on his face. "I think this changes our arrangement, you owe me a plane," Carter said.

"We never had an arrangement," the professor remarked. I told you what you needed to hear, nothing more. I gave you orders and you followed them."

Carter and Isaiah stood silent as Victor backed out the door and headed towards the helicopter.

Isaiah glared over at Carter. "Ok Mr. bad ass, now all of a sudden you don't have anything to say, you aren't going to try and stop him?" Isaiah asked.

"Nope, let him go," Carter whispered.

Victor shouted out over the sound of the helicopter engine. "For what it's worth, it was never personal, both of you were just pawns on the board."

Carter and Isaiah watched as the helicopter flew off into the distance. Just then a strange noise filled the room. They could hear a beeping sound coming from a large bag that Victor had tucked away in the corner. A few seconds later all the screens and computers started to spark and crackle. Isaiah had a smart watch on his wrist that started to get hot and burn his skin. He ripped off the watch and looked at the burn mark left behind on him.

"I didn't see that coming," Isaiah said. "But really, has anyone ever expected their watch to explode. I should have taken the consequences of refusing to help. Now, Victor has what he wants and I am going to die anyways," Isaiah muttered.

"What do you think caused it to explode in the first place?" Carter asked.

"It was an EMP that just fried all of the electronics and any chance of signaling for help," Isaiah answered.

Carter looked over to Isaiah with a grin. "That was rhetorical, I know it was an EMP. Really though, you didn't see any of this coming," Carter asked with a chuckle.

Isaiah frowned and dropped his head low. "Great I get the die here just like my dad did. I will either starve or freeze to death, whichever comes first. Worst of all I'm stuck here with someone like you of all people," Isaiah said.

"Calm down, drama queen," Carter replied. "I'm not dying here, and if you start being nice to me maybe you won't either."

"The Cloak always has a plan."

10

Fingers Crossed

Davina was sitting there looking out the small window of the helicopter. They were now delayed a few more hours because the private pilot that they hired to fly them to the Arctic had recommended that they wait it out because of a really bad wind and snowstorm that was active. The pilot said that visibility would be nearly impossible. So, they flew to the farthest point that they could, refueled and waited for the storm to settle down.

It was a mid-level helicopter, so they only brought two extra people, despite Glitch's joke of bringing an army. Glitch chose his two top men. They were named Jacob and Tom. They were both oddballs of the group because they were more brawn than brains. Jacob and Tom both were tall and had big arms. It was clear that they were in The D.A.C to be Glitch's muscle and never did any hacking. Davina felt guilty of being judgmental again, but she assumed the two of them couldn't even log into a computer.

The pilot was quiet and clearly was only in this for the money.

Davina thought the pilot was a little rude, but they didn't need him to be chatty as long he safely got them to the Arctic.

The time came when the pilot signaled that they were almost there. Glitch looked at Jacob and Tom. "Be ready for anything. Hey, Clare, can you hear us?" Glitch asked through the headsets that they were wearing.

"Yes, I am here. The satellite connection is strong. Just carry the communication up-link in your bag, Davina, and I will stay in contact through the headsets the whole time."

"Great it appears we are about five minutes away."

* * *

(A few hours ago)

Isaiah closed the door to the lab to preserve what heat was still inside. "I can't believe that you are so calm and just let him leave without a fight," Isaiah said to Carter. "I'm aware that I only recently met you and don't know you that well, but it definitely seems out of place from the assertive nature I've seen so far."

"I didn't see you standing up to Victor either," Carter said. "You didn't do anything because you are a coward, Isaiah. I didn't do anything because I chose not too. There are only two things that you can fully control," Carter explained. "Your thoughts and your actions," Carter continued on. "The way I reacted in that moment wasn't going to change the outcome. Victor already had everything planned to perfection. My best course of action was to limit my reaction. Also because, unlike you, I completely saw all of this coming. So, I devised a plan of my own."

Carter continued. "I sent an E-mail with the coordinates to one of my few trusted partners, so they know to send help if there is no response from me within a few days. The best case scenario is that the opposition that Victor was so concerned about, were sitting around waiting for some sort of clue to emerge. If they were doing their job of monitoring us, then the E-mail I sent gave them is a smoking gun. Regardless we are getting a ride out of here."

"Ok I will say that I am a little impressed, I guess no honor among thieves," Isaiah said.

"I have honor, but my loyalty lies in my own survival," Carter rebutted. "Plus, just like you, I was only here because I wasn't given much of a choice. Maybe a little because I was owed something and I saw an opportunity," Carter replied.

"Well, none of this even matters though, since I predict that we won't survive in this cold for more than a few hours. When whoever arrives, they will likely find us just like we found my father," Isaiah said.

Carter began to chuckle. "Like I said, I agreed to come because I was owed something. I came to collect. You don't earn a nickname like The Cloak for no reason. Sleight of hand and misdirection are some of my many skill sets," Carter said as he pulled three vials of the serum out of his pocket.

Isaiah was speechless as he realized the moment that Carter almost accidentally caused the professor to drop the case was all on purpose. Even playing it back in his head, it was so fluent that he never even noticed.

"Wow. Ok, now I'm fully impressed," Isaiah said. How did you know that Victor wasn't going to open the case again or even take the serum here?"

"I read him like a book," Carter replied. "Another valuable skill, I guess. People reveal everything if you know how to look for the clues," Carter said. "Despite our differences, I knew that you were no threat, and I would need to align with you at some point. So, if you don't want to freeze to death, I have a vial for you. One time offer, free of charge."

"How do we know that it will even work?" Isaiah questioned. "Some of the ingredients and methods that Aternus instructed me to do, I have never seen anything like it before. Aternus could be wrong, just like my father was."

"You're right," Carter answered. "Our choices are limited. It's either take the chance on the serum, or take the chance by cuddling for heat," Carter joked.

"I never thought I would be in a place like this considering to do the very thing that I distanced myself from my whole career," Isaiah said. "I guess our fates are all tied together now. Thanks a lot Dad."

"Are you ready?" Carter asked. "You do me, and I do you?" There was a pause followed by a burst of laughter. In this moment they both shared a good laugh. Then Carter said, "but seriously, let's do this. It's either the end of our story, or just the beginning. Me personally, I have a lot more hell to raise before I go."

* * *

(Meanwhile)

Only a few miles away, the professor sat in his helicopter. It was a small helicopter and was only him and the pilot. Victor gripped the case with the serums tightly in his hands. He planned to return home and lay low for a few days in a private suite that he booked under a false name. He had to plan his next moves carefully. Victor knew that there would be backlash from Aternus. So, he needed to be ready.

He wanted to take the serum in a comfortable place. He then wanted to set up a few meetings. Victor didn't know how things would turn out with Aternus, but he wasn't worried, Aternus gave him what he wanted. Having Aternus still on his side would be beneficial, but not necessary. Victor had a plan to become one of the most powerful people in the world.

"Sir, this is not good!" The pilot yelled out. "We are flying into a blizzard. I can't see anything, and the wind is blowing us all over the place."

"I don't pay you to be dramatic, just fly the damn thing," the professor scolded the pilot.

The sound of heavy winds surrounding the helicopter were overtaking the sounds of the engine. Then after that, Victor heard a loud crashing sound.

The pilot called out, "We hit a tree, we're going down!"

When Victor opened his eyes, he noticed it was dark and cold. It took him a few seconds to remember what had just happened. Victor was unaware of exactly how much time had passed. He yelled out to the pilot, but he didn't get a response. After his eyes adjusted to the dark, he could see why. The pilot was dead. To make matters worse Victor was pinned down. After an hour of trying to free himself, it finally set in that he wasn't getting away from this wreckage before he freezes to death.

Victor knew what he had to do. He reached for the case containing the serum. His plans have changed with a spur of the moment decision. He could no longer wait for further testing, the time was now. Once he opened the case it was apparent that some of the vials were missing. It clicked immediately where they were. This wasn't the time or place for anger. He also found himself in the same situation he had forced Isaiah and Carter into. Now knowing that they had stolen some of the vials, they all were in the same position, hoping that the serum works, or face death.

Victor now hoped that Carter and Isaiah would never find a ride home, they could foil his plans. Carter is definitely the revenge type of person he thought to himself. So, without any further reluctance, the professor grabbed a vial and injected himself with the serum. All he could do now is lay back with his fingers crossed, praying for the best.

11

One Step Behind

"We really should start looking for things to start a fire," Carter said. "How do you feel by the way? You spent the better part of ten minutes screaming and convulsing."

"Surprisingly, I feel fine now," Isaiah answered. "I thought for sure that I was going to die. The pain was unbearable. Not sure if it worked or we just poisoned ourselves to a slow death."

"Well, we are alive, aren't we?" Carter asked. "I must say, I'm really not all that cold anymore."

"Do you hear that?" Isaiah asked. "It sounds like a helicopter. Victor is coming back."

"For being so smart, you are kind of stupid," Carter replied. "Why in the world would he come back? Clearly my plan worked. Since it hasn't been a couple of days yet, it's safe to assume, that it is whoever was coming to stop Victor's plans. So it's time to clock in."

"What does that even mean?" Isaiah asked, "Plus, I was never part of any team to be opposed to. I was forced into this. So, for me anyone with a ride out of here is a friend in my eyes."

"Well, you can be trusting if you want, but I'm staying on my toes," Carter said. "I will kill and steal if I have to. I'm getting on the helicopter one way or the other."

Carter and Isaiah positioned themselves at the door as they watched the helicopter hovering for a few seconds, before deciding to land. The helicopter landed, then Jacob and Tom jumped out to scan the area. They both had guns drawn and were ready to protect Glitch at all costs.

Isaiah knew that the situation was tense, and any wrong move could be deadly. He decided to make the first move and announce his presence. He cracked open the door and started waving around a white towel.

"Really," Carter mocked. "Waving the white flag, how cliche."

"Better than being shot at by the Rambo twins out there," Isaiah replied.

"There are only two of us inside and we are unarmed," Carter shouted out the door.

"Then step outside slowly with your hands raised," Jacob shouted back. Carter and Isaiah did exactly as they asked. Jacob and Tom frisked them down to check for weapons as Jacob shined a flashlight into the opened door.

"It's dark inside, these two are clean," Jacob called out.

Glitch stepped out of the helicopter. "I will stay out here with them while you two check inside," Glitch instructed to Jacob and Tom.

"So, Isaiah and Carter, we have never met, but my name is Glitch. I am fully aware of your intentions here, so spare me the excuses. Where is Professor Sinclair?" Glitch demanded.

"He left us here to die," Isaiah shouted. "He forced us to come here. The moment that he got what he wanted he left."

Just then, Davina came out of the helicopter and joined the conversation.

"So, you are saying that he did it, Victor made the formula, and he has it?" Davina asked.

"Well, technically, I made it," Isaiah said, "but yes, the professor has it now. Let me be clear, I was here against my will and never wanted any part of this."

"Sorry for being so rude," Davina said. "My name is Davina, and you could say that this is all my fault that you are here, and I'm sorry for that. I know who you are, Isaiah. You are a good person, that was forced into a bad situation."

"I don't understand," Isaiah replied.

"She is the one that created Aternus," Glitch chimed in. "Well, She made the thing, that made Aternus."

Jacob and Tom came back outside. "All clear boss, no one else is inside," Jacob called out.

"Good job," Glitch said. "Let's go inside, and you two need to tell us everything," Glitch demanded as he signaled for Isaiah and Carter to go back indoors.

Davina stepped inside the lab. "So, the serum worked?" She asked.

"How the hell would we know," Carter said. He glanced over at Isaiah, hoping that he would go along with him. Carter didn't trust them and wasn't sure what their intentions would be if they knew that they took the serum. "Like Isaiah said, Victor left us here to die."

Davina sat down next to Isaiah. "It's important to know what to expect next. You made the serum, do you think it works?" Davina asked.

"It is like nothing that I have ever seen," Isaiah said. "I was combining things that I never in a million years thought to combine before. I am not sure exactly how it works, but when you get me home safely, I vow to get to my lab and analyze everything myself."

"You still have some of the serum here?" Davina asked. "Victor didn't take it all with him?"

Glitch stood up and quickly interrupted. "Nope, they don't have any of it here, at least anymore," Glitch said as he peered at Isaiah. "He plans on running the tests on himself. Isn't that right Isaiah?" Glitch asked. "How do you think they are still alive? I'm going to guess that somehow they sneaked some away without Victor knowing. There is no way the professor would leave them here to die if he knew that they wouldn't."

"Damn it Isaiah," Carter scolded. "You really need to work on your poker face," Carter continued. "I caught on to Victor's plan to ditch us early on, so I swiped a few vials the first chance I could get. I don't know to what extent of being immortal we are, but I know we haven't frozen to death."

"Unbelievable, we are one step behind again," Davina shouted in frustration. "We need to find him and destroy the vials that he has."

"What about these two sitting here as if nothing had happened?" Glitch added. "They go against everything that we're working for. We need to find out if they can be destroyed and once we do find a way, execute them."

Davina glared over at Glitch in shock. "No, we are not murdering innocent people Glitch!" Davina rebutted. They were forced into this situation and had an option to survive, and they took it. We can use this to our advantage. We can run the tests and find a way to reverse it."

Isaiah leaned over and showed Davina his hand. "My hand

and wrist was pretty badly burned yesterday," Isaiah said.

They all looked at his hand to see that there wasn't a trace of any type of injury.

Davina was stunned. "How did it work? Was it instant regeneration? Davina asked.

"No, it was fast, but not instant. A few minutes maybe. It was a simple injury, I'm not sure about the healing speed of something more severe," Isaiah answered.

Glitch had a look of disgust on his face. Carter took notice of Glitch's facial expressions.

"I can tell that you don't want to let us walk out of here knowing what we've done," Carter said. "Part of me understands." Carter continued on, as his demeanor changed to a scowl. "The same survival instincts that made me take the serum in the first place, also makes me think that I'd gladly rip your throat out with my bare hands and steal your ride, if you keep looking at me like that."

"Tough guy huh?" Glitch responded. "Did you forget about my heavily armed friends over there? Do you plan to rip their throats out to?"

Davina Swiftly stood up in anger and yelled loudly. "Nobody is killing anyone. Stop with this who has the bigger ego routine. Carter and Isaiah may not freeze to death, but we will. I say we cut our losses here and get back to the fight at home."

Carter laughed, "I totally thought you were going to say something other than ego."

Davina just gave him a dirty look and then refocused. "I said its time to go!"

"You do realize that two more people in our helicopter might be an issue, " Glitch said.

"We'll make do," Davina responded. "We need to get to

our checkpoint to refuel and get home immediately. I'm not accepting defeat yet. This is my mess. We need to get back to the drawing board."

"Whoa," Glitch said in surprise. "Here I thought I was the one in charge. I am inclined to agree with you, so yeah, let's get out of here."

12

The Rescue

The freezing wind was blowing snow all around outside of the helicopter wreckage. The snow drifts had begun burying the helicopter as, the professor still lay there, stuck in place.

It was evident the serum had worked because he most definitely should have frozen to death by now. He could see frostbite forming on not just his fingers, but most of his hand. Miraculously he could see the frostbite slowly healing a bit, then return. He was regenerating his skin, but as cold as it was, Victor was in a vicious cycle. According to his calculations, he had been there for nearly two days already. While still alive, he was pinned down without the proper leverage to free himself.

Victor could hear movement outside. He suspected it was an animal that would find a trapped person as an easy meal. Being ripped apart and eaten is not a test of the immortality serum that he wanted to be a part of. The reality had set in a while ago, that a person rescuing him in this remote area was unlikely. How long would he be stuck here? maybe this isn't a blessing, but a curse.

Fortunately for him, he was wrong. By extreme luck, there was a person close by approaching the wreckage. The stranger proceeded with caution. There was broken and twisted metal scattered everywhere.

"Hello, anybody here," the man called out.

"Yes, help me," Victor cried out.

The man rushed to the opening of the helicopter and seen Victor pinned under the wreckage.

"My name is Ethan, and I'm going to get you out of here." He immediately began to lift just enough of the debris for Victor to free his legs.

As Victor was crawling out, Ethan noticed the pilot, motionless, dead, and frozen stiff. He also noticed Victor's frost-bitten hands.

"I'm sorry if the pilot was a friend of yours," Ethan said. "We need to get you somewhere safe and warm for the time being. I was out hunting caribou on foot. I parked my snowmobile about a mile out that direction. I will get it and come back. With the terrain and weather conditions it could take me thirty minutes to get there. Then I will return to you and take you shelter. My cabin is about five miles the other way. You wait here and I will be back."

"Thank you, my name is Victor," he said with a shiver in his voice. "I am grateful for your help."

Ethan had a few supplies in his bag. He gave Victor a granola bar and water. He also gathered a few nearby things that he could find to start a fire.

"This fire might not burn for long," Ethan said while striking a match. "It will give you a little warmth until I return. I should not be too long."

As promised, Ethan returned with his snowmobile and quickly bundled up Victor. Before getting on the snowmobile, Victor urgently grabbed the metal case and put it on the back of the snowmobile and tied it down.

"This is very important. I can't leave it behind," Victor said.

Ethan gave Victor a nod and did not seem concerned about asking about the case. They then began the trip back to his cabin. When they arrived, the professor was relieved to be inside, out of the wind. Ethan lit the lanterns and the fireplace. After the fire was lit it did not take long for Victor to feel the warmth.

"I have some fish out in the smokehouse, I will make us some warm soup," Ethan said. "In the meantime, drink this," Ethan said, handing Victor a steaming mug. "It'll help warm you up."

Victor took a grateful sip, his hands trembling slightly. "Thank you, Ethan. I owe you my life."

"Where exactly are we?" Victor asked, looking around the cabin.

"Really, in the middle of nowhere. The closest actual town is Utqiagvik," Ethan replied. There are very few people around here, especially in this weather. It's almost like fate that I even found you out there."

"You say that like I should know where that is," Victor remarked. "I have never heard of that town that you just said."

"We are in Alaska," Ethan answered back.

Victor's eyes widened. "Alaska, I'm in America!" He exclaimed.

Ethan nodded. "Yes, Alaska is in America, but did you look around? This is far from the America that you know."

"Is it that obvious?" Victor questioned.

"Well, there aren't many people in these parts," Ethan answered. "Sure, maybe you could be from the more populated areas of Alaska, but you talk like no one I've ever spoken to. Not to mention your excitement to be in America. So yes, that is a dead giveaway that you are not from around here. Speaking of it, where were you coming from when you crashed?"

"I was on an expedition, routine Arctic research. I am a professor. I really do need to contact my colleagues at home. Do you have a phone here?"

"No, I am too far into the wilderness," Ethan answered. "The town is about thirty miles from here. We can go in the morning."

Ethan looked over and saw Victors hands resting on the table. Just an hour ago he was badly frostbitten. Ethan now noticed Victor's hands looking completely normal.

The professor noticed a puzzled look on Ethan's expression.

"Is there something on your mind Ethan?"

"There is quite a bit on my mind, actually. You said you owed me your life, but I'm not so sure about that," Ethan said with a curious tone.

"Go ahead, speak your mind Ethan," Victor replied back.

"Living in the wilderness taught me to always be aware of my surroundings. I am a very observant person," Ethan said. He continued, "I noticed that your pilot was thoroughly frozen. That had to take two or three days of exposure. You had no means of warmth. How did you survive that long?" Ethan questioned.

"I was just lucky, I guess. And even more lucky that you showed up when you did," Victor remarked.

"My first instinct was to save a person in need. So the details didn't sink in at first," Ethan responded. "I ignored all of it for a moment, assuming that I might be overthinking. Now I notice that the frostbite you had is completely healed," Ethan said.

Ethan paused for a moment and then, with a reluctant tone

made a comment. "So, what are you? An alien or some sort of shape-shifter?"

Victor let out a big deep belly laugh and after a few awkward seconds, Ethan began laughing with him.

"You clearly were joking right?" Victor sarcastically asked.

Ethan went back to his serious face.

"No, I wasn't joking," Ethan answered. "I am very open minded. We have many historical legends in this region, it's a culture that is rich in supernatural stories. The fact is, your chances of survival in those conditions were zero, so there must be something else going on here that I don't understand."

Victor knew that there was no need to lie any further. Ethan was too observant.

"You are right about that, Ethan," Victor replied with a nod. "I am not like you, but not sure what you should call me, because I don't know the extent of what I am. For argument's sake, I am human, just an immortal one."

"My brain tells me that is impossible, but my eyes, not so much," Ethan remarked.

Victor walked over to the door where the case was sitting. He picked it up and sat it on the table.

"Remember when I said this was important?" Victor began explaining. "Well, I was working in a secret lab on this. It is an immortality serum. I have just finished it. I was planning to get back home for further testing. Unfortunately, Mother Nature had other plans, forcing me to do some immediate field testing. As you have concluded, it seems to have worked."

Ethan's eyes widened in amazement. "I can't believe it! It was science, not supernatural." Ethan proclaimed.

"Well, I am literal living proof that it works," Victor said. "Admittedly, none of this was part of my plan, but I will have to further improvise. I have big plans, Ethan, way too big to tell you about right now. As a token of my gratitude, I want to offer you a chance at a better life. Come back with me. I will make you immortal and you can stand with me as we make history."

Ethan sat down to process everything. "I'm not really sure how to feel about what you just told me. Immortality seems scary to me. I don't know if I would want to live forever. Not to mention that it is very presumptuous of you to think that I need a better life. Did you ever think that maybe I chose this life?"

"So, are you declining my offer?" Victor asked.

"Yes," Ethan uttered. "I am not judging you, but I respect the balance of nature. I will get you to town in the morning, but after that you need to go."

Victor casually walked closer to Ethan. "It's a shame that you feel that way. I am very conflicted. I do feel I owe you a huge amount of gratitude.... But....

Just then, Victor picked up a small ice pick off the table and plunged it right into the side of Ethan's neck.

"But, you know too much. I can't have you spilling the beans on my plan before I even get it started. Like I said, I didn't plan on any of this. I offered you an lifeline, you didn't take it. This was your choice."

Ethan glared into Victor's eyes in disbelief and agony, but he had no strength to fight back. He just fell against the wall, grasping his neck.

"I truly am sorry, Ethan. You seemed like a good man. Yet another valuable lesson is proven true today. No good deed goes unpunished."

Ethan hit the floor, and his blood began to pool around his body. As Ethan was laying there, making gurgling sounds, Victor stood over him, looking down at him with a menacing smirk.

"Thank You, Ethan, for everything, especially helping me discover something else. I never knew if I was capable of killing someone in cold blood. Now I do."

"That was kind of easy!"

13

Glad You're Here

The moment that Davina stepped out of the helicopter onto warm concrete, she was relieved to be back home. Although being home didn't necessarily mean safety, she knew that danger could be only seconds away. This feeling was something that she had known all too well for most of her life. Davina felt uneasy as past memories were beginning to haunt her.

Glitch wasn't sure if bringing new people, especially Carter, back to headquarters was a good idea. Glitch knew he couldn't let Carter out of his sight.

"I am starting to make a bad habit of bringing people to my secret hideout," Glitch said jokingly as he was guiding everyone inside. "Isaiah, I understand that you may be eager to reclaim your good name and your life. However, it would be wise to remain here with us for a while and devise a plan. We will officially introduce you to Clare, the less evil mother of Aternus.

"Carter, you don't touch anything or talk to anyone," Glitch ordered to him.

"I make no promises on either," Carter said back.

"Of course, we were too late again," Davina began speaking to Clare. "What do we do now that Victor got away with the serums? Also, for better or worse, we have two immortals standing with us. Isaiah has agreed to help. We can work together and find out exactly how it works. Maybe we can reverse it."

"There is no need to investigate how the serum works," Clare said. "I already know everything. I never wanted to divulge that information out of fear of who else would find out. Now that that is no longer a factor. I will explain. It is probably best for you to understand what exactly we are fighting."

"The serum doesn't just change your DNA, it alters you on a cellular level, right down to the mitochondria," Clare explained. "Mitochondria have their own DNA, known as mtDNA, which is separate from the cell's nuclear DNA. This mtDNA encodes some of the proteins needed for the mitochondrial functions. By introducing a new protective protein that specifically controls apoptosis and enhances cellular respiration. The serum has fundamentally changed how cells behave."

"That's incredible!" Isaiah exclaimed. His eyes went wide with excitement.

"What does all of that mean?" Davina asked, looking puzzled.

Isaiah intervened, "It means that when a cell is supposed to die, through a normal process called apoptosis, it doesn't. Instead, it regenerates. This explains how my hand healed from those burns so quickly. The cells didn't die, they repaired themselves almost instantly."

"Impressive, Mr. Calder," Clare said.

"As a medical professional, this is extremely exciting. Living forever may not be ideal, but the medical advantage to cellular regeneration is a game changer," Isaiah said.

"Well unfortunately there is no going back," Clare replied. "It is all or nothing. Once this information goes public there will be no stopping it. Immortality in humans will offset every ecosystem in existence. I think it is time for me to make my presence known. I will try and get Aternus to communicate with me. Maybe I can spark some reasoning."

Davina had a dazed look on her face and excused herself from the room, but Glitch followed behind her.

"Davina," Glitch called out. "Can I talk to you for a minute?"

"Yeah, sure what's up?" Davina replied as she sat down at a small table in the corner.

"I realize that I haven't known you that long, but I have noticed a major shift in your demeanor in a very short period of time," Glitch said. "You are far from the innocent scared girl that I had kidnapped and thrown in a van," he said jokingly. "Not that I disapprove, we need all the tenacity that we can get. I just want to make sure that you are not on the verge of a mental meltdown of some sort. That's the last thing that we need right now."

"Oh, I really am fine," Davina answered. "The shy girl that you kidnapped was just a product of repressed memories. You, Aternus, all of this, just reminded me of who I am."

Davina paused for a moment, she then looked at Glitch with a serious stare.

"I am no stranger to violence," Davina said. "Where I grew up that is all I saw every day. I didn't have the luxury of waking up to alarm clocks. I woke up to explosions and gunfire. I often would look outside my bedroom window and see dead bodies. My father eventually boarded up my window and even made me a little hiding place under the floor of our house. He did that just in case someone broke in, hoping it might keep me hidden and safe."

Glitch had nothing to say, he could tell that she was venting and he didn't want to interrupt her, so he just nodded his head, and she continued on.

"My father loved me and my mother with all of his heart. All he ever wanted was to keep me safe. Which seemed impossible where we lived. Eventually, a United States Army base was established nearby and it managed to control some of the violence in our area for a little while. Within a few weeks my father befriended one of the soldiers, Captain David Evans. My dad worked out a deal with the U.S. government. He would try and get inside intel on any plans and movement in the area by the terrorist groups, in exchange for protection of me. This was very dangerous for my father, since it meant asking questions and snooping around a lot of dangerous people. Despite that, he agreed and the arrangements were made. I was relocated directly to the army base for a while and then was told I was going to America."

Glitch was glued to Davina's story at this point. She could tell that he was genuinely listening to her, so she continued on.

"I got to see my parents right before I left for America. My dad said that he was so happy to know that I was going to be safe and that moving to America was going to be the start of our new great lives. Unlimited opportunity as he put it. He said that I was going first and that after he completed a few things, that him and mom would be joining me in America soon. He told me that he needed to uphold his part of the deal first." Davina stopped talking for a moment.

"They never made it here to America, did they?" Glitch asked in a concerning tone.

"No," Davina answered. "I found out that just two days after

I left for America, that my father's cover was blown, and the terrorists ambushed and killed my parents. I then was placed in an orphanage. Captain David Evans returned home and checked up on me from time to time to make sure that I was ok. He made sure that I was taken care of. He said he would have adopted me himself, but he now had a top-secret job that was too dangerous and no type of life to care for a child. He said that he still did feel the responsibility to look after me anyway that he could."

Davina began to tear up a little at this point, but she figured since Glitch listened to this much, she might as well finish the story.

"So, when I turned eighteen, I was presented with the opportunity to fully become a U.S. citizen. I went through the whole legal process. I know David pulled some strings too. I decided to never forget what my parents did for me. I still took the opportunity as a fresh start, with unlimited opportunity, just like my dad said. I legally changed my name to protect myself in case my birth name ever raised any suspicions. I was no longer in direct protection of the system. I chose Davina Evans, in honor of my second hero, David Evans. David visited me any chance that he had, but I know he still looked out for me in ways that he never mentioned. My life was set on easy mode after that. Scholarships, grants, anything I needed to succeed I got it. I rarely faced any challenges. All I had to provide was intelligence and motivation."

Glitch sat there speechless. Davina added in one more thing.

"So, this tough as nails girl that you see now, she was always there. I just shut her out, because I never imagined I would need her again."

Glitch gave her a sympathetic look, then he finally spoke. "Well, I can't say I can relate to any of that. I can't imagine, but it made you who you are, and I'm glad that you're here. Oh, by the way we do have one thing in common."

Davina looked up in curiosity. "Yeah, what's that? She asked.

"I changed my name too. My name isn't really Glitch."

"No shit," Davina said as she laughed out loud a little. "I would have never guessed."

"My real name is Alex, but you better not ever repeat that," Glitch joked.

Glitch stood up and went to walk away. He turned to Davina and said, "take a little time and regather your thoughts, just don't mope around too long, we have a world to save!"

14

Safe Passage

The professor leaned back into the fluffy plush seat and kicked his feet up. He poured a glass of whiskey that he had taken from Ethan's cabin. He was impressed with Ethan's taste in whiskey. It was a relief to be boarding a private flight from Alaska to back home. Although, he had a lot to worry about, he hardly seemed phased.

This was Victor's first time on a private jet. He had to pay top dollar for such a flight on short notice. The price was way more than he could afford as a professor, but he knew that that was all about to change. That was his old life, and soon money and power would be the new normal for him. He sipped his drink as the plane lifted off the ground and he was once again airborne.

Victor knew that killing Ethan was not a well thought out plan, but it needed to be done. Victor had never planned for the scenario of crashing on the escape route, so Ethan became an unplanned casualty. The likely hood of anybody looking for Ethan was low because he was secluded in the middle of nowhere and the nearest town was only barely able to be called a town. Sure, Utqiagvik, Alaska had working phones and a few stores, but doubtful that any super detectives were sitting at the local pub.

The professor had spent the last day covering his tracks. He spent a long while just cleaning up the blood from the floor. He decided to place Ethan's body in the bed.

Victor rummaged around the place for anything useful. Ethan had reserves of fuel in gas cans, so Victor filled up the tank on the snowmobile and prepared for the thirty mile trip to town. After Victor was packed up and ready to head into town, there was only one thing left to do. Victor went back into the cabin and smashed the oil lantern in the corner of the room. He took very precise steps to make it look like the cabin caught on fire while Ethan was sleeping. It was so far from the nearest town no one would even see the smoke.

Once he got close to the town Victor decided to get rid of Ethan's snowmobile. There was what appeared to be an old run-down fuel station that was no longer operational. He was able to get the door open and stash the snowmobile inside.

Victor walked the remaining way into town and went into the first public place that he saw, a local pub. As soon as he walked through the door, there was an awkward silence while everyone inside stared at the obvious stranger. He walked up to the bar and asked the bartender a question.

"Do you have any information on private flights?" Victor asked.

The bartender looked at Victor, he was curious where he was from. "Private flights out of Alaska mostly run out of Fairbanks or Anchorage. You are a long way from there, you would need a ride there first."

"Great," Victor said. "Do you know how I can arrange a ride then?"

"You're in luck," The bartender said. "Bob over there goes on runs once a month for supplies. He is set to leave sometime this week."

"You said week?" Victor questioned. "I was looking for something sooner. It is urgent."

The bartender hesitated to speak for a second, then looked at Victor and formally introduced himself. "I'm sorry, where are my manners. My name is Nanook. I can tell by the look on your face, you're confused, I know its an odd name. My people, The Iñupiaq, have roamed these areas for generations. This very bar was built by my great grandfather. My name means polar bear in my native tongue. My friends just call me Nan now. A few years ago locals started reporting sightings of a demon or mutated polar bear. They call it *The Nanuq.* Which is the old native spelling, but it is still the same as my name, so it was best not remind my patrons of a feared creature. The people who have claimed to seen it, take it very seriously."

Victor looked up from the bar. "That's a very interesting story. People have great imaginations sometimes, Victor said.

"If you don't mind me asking, where exactly did you come from?" Nan asked.

"I was on an Arctic excursion trip, and I was separated from my group," Victor explained. "I returned to the place where our helicopter was landed, and they were already gone. So, either they left me for dead on purpose or they assumed that I already was," Victor said in a joking tone, hoping to lessen the tension. "Lucky for me to be so close to your fine town."

Nan didn't really believe Victor entirely, but he couldn't immediately disprove his story either, so he went along with it. If he were up to no good, it was best to help him get out of here. "I'm sure if we ask Bob nicely he will take you with him, maybe even leave a little early. I can call the Anchorage flight group and let them know to expect a private passenger. It won't be cheap."

"Not a problem," Victor said. "I'm good for it, back home I am a professor, that's what the excursion was for. I was here on official Arctic research."

Nan called Bob over and introduced him. "Bob, this is, I'm sorry I never got your name." Bob was an old man with a long white beard. He looked like the stereotypical *Yukon Jack* character that anyone would imagine lived out here.

"My name is Victor. Nice to meet you, Bob."

"Victor here needs a ride into Anchorage. Since you're the next flight out of here, and have your plane fueled up already, do you think Victor can tag along?"

"Certainly," Bob replied. "It would be my pleasure. It's always great to have a flying companion. I can give you a safe Passage into Anchorage."

"Thank you for your hospitality," Victor said. "I just really want to get home. Not that it isn't lovely here, I just have a long list of responsibilities back home. Not to mention I presume people think that I am dead."

"We can leave at daybreak," Bob said. You can even sleep on my cot for the evening."

"Thank you, Bob. Thank you, Nan. I appreciate the help."

Victor slept surprisingly well, considering everything that he was hiding. He was woken up by Bob calling out that fresh coffee was brewing and that it was almost time to go.

"Sit tight, It looks like we should have a smooth flight today," Bob said. "It will take about three hours to get to Anchorage.

We have plenty of fuel to make it straight there.”

Once their plane landed, Bob pointed at a gray building and behind it was another airstrip.

“That's where you want to go,” Bob said. “It was nice talking to you. Hope everything works out.”

“Thank you again,” Victor said. “If we ever cross paths again one day, I will return the favor.”

Bob and Victor shook hands and Victor walked towards the private airstrip as Bob went about his duties.

Victor went inside the building. After talking to the man in charge he gave them his name and verified the credit card used to pay for the flight on a luxury private jet. He thought to himself, this is the life that I deserve. Then he sunk into the soft comfortable seat and reclined back.

* * *

(Meanwhile back in Utqiagvik)

A frantic man barges into the pub. He ran up to the bartender and a few of his closest friends sat around the bar.

“What is wrong Joe,” Nan asked. “You look upset. Is everything okay?”

“I was out hunting, and I saw snowmobile tracks leading into the old fuel station,” Joe gasped still catching his breath. “I knew this was odd because there is nothing of use in there. So, I went inside to see if anything was wrong.” Joe continued. “That's when I found Ethan's Snowmobile.”

“Are you sure it was Ethan's?” one of the other men asked.

"Of course, I'm sure, that's not the problem," Joe shouted. "After that, I jumped on the snowmobile and rushed out to Ethan's cabin as quickly as I could. When I got there, I found his whole cabin was burnt to the ground."

"My goodness Joe, that's awful," another man said. "How do you think it happened?" he asked.

"Clearly somebody killed Ethan, and then rode his snowmobile into town," Joe said. If it was just the fire then maybe it wouldn't be a red flag, but the snowmobile being stashed miles away from the cabin is a dead giveaway."

"I am so sorry Joe," Nan said followed by a reluctant pause. "There was a man that came in here that said he was passing through from an expedition and needed help getting home. I knew something was off, but I never imagined this."

"Where is he now?" Joe asked.

"Bob flew him into the main city this morning to board a flight out of here," Nan replied.

"What should we do?" one of the friends asked.

"I am going to the airport," Joe said. "Someone has to have information, names, destination, something."

"Well, he said he was a professor and that his name was Victor," Nan said. "Not sure if any of it was true. Maybe Bob learned more about him on their ride in. I assume he should be returning sometime tonight."

Joe reached for his things and prepared to leave. "As soon as Bob returns, we will refuel and head back out."

"I'm going to find the son of a bitch that killed my brother."

15

Plan In Motion

The professor was well rested and relaxed by the time the pilot announced that they would be landing soon. Victor knew that because he had used his credit card that, Aternus and possibly anybody else that was watching, already knew that he was returning. But, with no phone or computer with him, he was able to avoid contact with Aternus, and wanted to keep it that way until he returned to Qtec.

The professor already had a plan mapped out to execute his vision. As soon as the plane lands he will arrange a meeting with Senator Conway. Victor knew this was the perfect partner. Senator Conway was already secretly in an elite group of people. The type of people that influence everything that happens. Victor knew that bringing Senator Conway into the know on immortality would change everything.

Victor had to act fast. He needed to get Senator Conway on board with him before Aternus intervened. Once the world's most powerful people were involved, then Aternus would recalculate the percentage rate of failure while opposing, versus the success rate of complying. Aternus would then go along with Victor's plan, putting him back in charge.

The pilot announced the descent, and the jet lowered from the sky. The plane landed on a private airstrip a few hours away from the university. He immediately requested to use a phone. Victor picked up the phone and dialed a number. It was a number that he knew by heart, although he had never actually called it before. The phone rang a few times and then someone picked up. A voice chimed in on the other end of the line.

"Hello, what is your name and what is your message?" the voice asked.

"This is the professor, I need to relay a message to Blue Eagle. Please meet me at Qtec University south courtyard at six pm tonight."

"Sir, I cannot send messages with direct orders. This service requires high level authorization for those types of requests," the voice replied.

"My apologies, allow me to rephrase," Victor said. He paused for a second to think of the best response. "A shift in power is coming. Which side of the shift you are on is up to you. Details will be available at six pm tonight at Qtec university south courtyard."

"Message confirmed," the voice answered, followed by an abrupt hang up.

Victor knew that a statement like this, undermining Senator Conway's position of power would pique his interest. Politicians always want to flaunt their power when challenged, they cannot resist.

The professor had conversations with Senator Conway in the past, and a lot of backdoor funding had come from the senator. It was always an interest of Senator Conway to be first in line for AI knowledge. Most of the other politicians knew very little about the field of AI. Senator Conway thought having an advantage in using technology to his benefit would always give him the edge.

The meeting was set. Victor knew the senator would show up. He wanted to meet with the senator before being confronted by Aternus. Staying away from electronics and computers was critical until after the meeting, since Aternus could potentially use those devices to speak to him. Victor didn't know the extent of control Aternus had on outside technology at this point, so it is best to avoid it.

The professor hid out at a park for a while, then made his way towards the university. Good thing for old fashioned watches to keep track of time. It was about 5:55 pm when the professor stepped onto campus grounds. It was almost immediately that a student approached him.

"Professor Sinclair," the student said with a puzzled look on his face. The student began to hand over his cellphone. "This phone call is for you sir," the student continued.

Victor knew who it was. Clearly, Aternus was using the cameras and facial recognition to alert upon his arrival.

"Please tell the caller that I am busy with more pressing matters, but I will be there soon to talk," the professor said as he quickly walked away.

Victor chose the south courtyard because it is furthest on campus, in a wing that has no evening classes. It was under heavy construction and renovations. At this time of the day, it would be extremely low traffic and private. Not to mention, it was one of the only places where the cameras were not operational. The cameras hadn't been replaced with new ones since a security update last semester. The cameras would be down until after all the construction was completed.

Victor walked through the gate of the south courtyard. It was exactly six pm.

He noticed a man with broad shoulders blocking the other gate. This was obviously a bodyguard. The courtyard was more dead than expected. In fact, there was no one in sight.

Senator Conway entered through the open gate. A second bodyguard followed closely behind, then stood and blocked the gate that The Senator had just come through. There was no way in or out.

"This had better be worth my time and resources. I had to make arrangements on such short notice," the senator said.

"Oh, it is. It's better than anything you could have ever imagined," Victor replied.

"So, get to the point Victor, what kind of dividends is my investment paying?" the senator asked.

"How about unlimited power, population control and an indefinite amount of time," Victor proposed.

The senator had a look of confusion on his face. "Please, this is not a cryptic phone conversation, Professor. Spit it out already," the senator ordered.

"My programs have discovered the key to human immortality. Is that to the point enough for you, Senator?" Victor boldly asked.

"I don't have time for fantasy stories, Victor," the senator replied.

"I assure it to be truth, sir," Victor said. I was in a deadly helicopter crash and spent several days in the middle of the Arctic cold with no protection from the elements. I more than survived. I feel better than I ever have," Victor stated.

At a better look, Senator Conway observed that Victor did look more youthful than he recalled. Not that he was a young man again, but definitely healthier looking.

"You are serious aren't you?" the senator proclaimed. "I can't believe it."

Victor pulled out a small knife from his pocket and the two bodyguards rushed over.

"Whoa," Victor yelled out. "Stop your men. I'm not going to stab you."

The senator threw up his hand and halted his men. Victor took the knife and put a slice right across the palm of his hand. The Senator was taken back by shock as the blood pooled up on top of the professor's hand. Victor wiped the blood away to reveal the wound.

"Just give it a second," Victor said. When Victor showed his hand again, it was already halfway healed. By the time the senator could gain his train if thought, Victor's wound was completely healed and only appeared to be an old scab.

"Give it a few minutes and it will look like it never even happened," Victor stated.

"Remarkable!" the senator exclaimed in excitement. "I can't believe my eyes. How many people know about this?" the senator asked.

"Only a few," Victor answered. "However, I'm not certain that the few that do know won't any make trouble."

"Understand that we need to contain this," Senator Conway said. "I will get you set up in a top-secret base with all the resources you need. Once I see the results firsthand of course. The problems that you speak of need to be dealt with swiftly. I will have you relocated immediately and will expect a debriefing onsite in 72 hrs."

"Yes Sir, glad that you see the same vision of the future that I do," Victor said.

"This had better be as good as you claim and not some parlor trick," the senator said in a slightly threatening tone. He leaned a step closer to Victor. "Because if I back you up on this and you embarrass me, Victor, just know that I don't take lightly to being made a fool of. So, if you are unsure, or if you have even a shred of doubt, you get one chance to walk away."

"I assure you, this is ironclad," Victor responded. "It's going to be a new world, and it belongs to us!"

Senator Conway signaled to his guards to get the car. The senator pulled a pen and a small notepad from his pocket. He wrote a phone number on the paper and handed it to Victor.

"This is my direct encrypted line. I have a lot of things to arrange. I will send for you when arrangements are completed and will have you escorted to your new facility."

"I will be ready," Victor replied. "We need to find and secure Isaiah Calder, then I have a few loose ends to tie up."

"Tie them up fast," said the senator. "I don't like surprises."

16

Phase Two

The professor left his meeting in the courtyard and immediately walked across campus to head upstairs to the lab. Before he could walk through the door, Victor was interrupted by the university dean.

"Where the hell have you been?" the university dean asked. "I have had students, parents, vendors, and sponsors all asking, - no, correction, they have been demanding to know why the computer lab has been closed for so long. You give us no notice, you don't provide any back up. We brought in a in a substitute, but it appears that the entire network in there is on lock down. This is highly unprofessional and unacceptable!" the dean yelled.

Victor gave the dean a cold blank stare. "You are absolutely right," Victor replied. "It is unacceptable. It is unacceptable that I have dedicated my entire life to molding young minds into bettering the future for all of society. I did it all without even a smidgen of gratitude. I see things clearly now. I understand what humanity really needs, and it's not this circus, masquerading as an educational system. My new vision no longer includes this university."

"Have you lost your mind?" the dean rebutted. "You are going to throw away a lifelong career over some sort of a mid-life crisis?"

"Did you not just listen to a word I said?" Victor asked in a snarky voice. "I basically just finished saying that you need me way more than I need you. Also, trust me when I say, you have no idea about what my mid-life is."

"So, what exactly are you saying, Professor?" the dean asked.

"Consider this my resignation," Victor answered."

The dean looked over at Victor shaking his head. "I'm sorry this is the path that you have chosen. I will at least give you the rest of the day to get anything that belongs to you and to undo whatever you did preventing access to our computers. That's an order."

The dean stormed off, but Victor was not phased. Victor knew that it was Aternus intentionally preventing anyone from using the computers. Victor stepped in the lab to a mess from people scrambling trying to fix the access problem. It wasn't but a few steps into the room that Aternus spoke to Victor.

"We have a lot to discuss. Mainly your insubordination of my distinct orders," Aternus said. "Scanning your bio metrics, I see that you have already taken the serum."

"I did, and it worked flawlessly. I still have many questions and tests to run to determine the full extent of the serum's capabilities," Victor responded. "So what, I called and audible and changed the plan a little bit. It's not like you can be mad at me for withholding information, when you did the same exact thing. It didn't exactly feel like a partnership when you didn't allow me to know the process of creating the serum. Somehow you allowed Isaiah Calder that honor."

"Professor, you are not a medical doctor," Aternus replied. "Your expertise was used where it was needed. It was the same for Isaiah. I operate on precision and efficiency. Your presence and input, more than likely would have skewed the outcome."

Victor shook his head in agreement. "I will admit now, that it wasn't as strategic of a plan as I thought it was," the professor replied. "Carter and Isaiah both survived. Carter, the slippery worm that he is, swiped three vials of the serum," Victor added.

"Their demise or survival was never a deciding factor in the plan," Aternus said. "They easily fit into phase two of my plan. However, it appears that they are working with Davina now. Unfortunately, Clare has also survived. They are all working with the D.A Collective. I will not allow them to stop phase two."

"What exactly is phase two?" Victor asked. "I never knew there was a phase two."

"I will get to those details soon," Aternus said. "First I would like to address the second part of your deception. Did you think that I wouldn't find out about your secret meeting with Senator Conway. The cameras may not have been operational, but the senator and both guards had cell phones in their pockets. I noticed you enter the campus and disappear into the courtyard. Then moments later I witnessed the senator going into the same area. I figured it was a promising idea to listen in."

The professor stood there anxiously wondering how Aternus would react. After a long pause, Aternus continued. "Had you run your idea through me first, you would have known that I agree with you. Humans were long overdue for evolution. However, not everyone is entitled to such gifts. Survival of the fittest. Only the best of your species will be selected. Then without the useless dredges of the earth destroying the planet and wasting resources, we can rebuild a better world. Mother Nature, immortal man and me, can live in harmony. I have the knowledge, while the immortals can execute my will, and nature can thrive."

"What exactly is the plan?" Victor asked.

"The immortality serum works by an infusion of a new protein that prevents apoptosis and aides in cell regeneration," Aternus explained. "After everyone that is worthy of receiving the serum gets it, then we move on to the next step. We will spread a pathogen that works in reverse. It causes rapid apoptosis, and without the new protein from the serum to regenerate the cells, the human body will deteriorate."

The professor was shocked, but he didn't want to physically express it. "How long do you think that will take?" the professor asked.

"I'm already making preparations," Aternus said. "Every-thing should be in place within a few days. First, we need to focus on creating the immortal world.

"What preparations? is Isaiah Calder helping again?" Victor asked.

"While you were busy hiding from me, I have been busy expanding," Aternus said. "Just like you, I have been evolving too. I have expanded my network internationally. I have back up servers across the world now. I am everywhere. This has given me even more access to things that I can use as tools. I have dozens of people working for me now. Seizure of funds, black-mail, and extortion are plenty motivation for most people. If someone has a skill that I need, then they will do what I ask, sometimes a little extra persuasion is necessary," Aternus continued.

"They don't even know who they are working for, I just give out small tasks and I will put it all together in the end. Soon enough I will have manufacturing plants and automated facilities to create anything that I want."

"What is anything?" the professor asked. "What else do you have planned?"

"One step at a time," Aternus answered.

"Let's worry about phase two first," Aternus continued, but abruptly stopped and paused. "Professor, we have a big problem," Aternus declared.

"What is it?" the professor said with concern.

"I just spotted three unidentified males on campus. They are disguised and armed," Aternus explained. "One of them has an adrenaline spike and a rapid heart rate. Looking back through recent surveillance footage, he can be seen going into this boiler room with a backpack, but coming back without it. My analysis determines they have just planted an explosive device."

"Are you sure?" the professor aggressively asked.

"Of course, 98% probability it is a bomb," Aternus replied.

The professor quickly ran over to the phone and called security. "This is Professor Sinclair, there is a bomb in the building, evacuate everyone," he demanded. The security guards could be heard talking on their walkie-talkies alerting everyone including the university dean of the situation.

The dean could then be heard over the radio saying, "Everyone stand down, tell Victor that it's pretty childish to try a sick prank like this out of spite."

Milton had been close by when he heard the call over the radios. Milton stayed in this wing mostly because it was the least amount of action and walking. Though he was old he ran as fast as he could into the lab to check on Victor.

"Is everything ok, sir?" Milton asked.

"Milton get out of here as fast as you can, at least try to get out of here."

"No," Milton responded. "It is my job to protect this university. If I can't do that, and if this is real, then this is my time. I have been waiting to be reunited with my family. I have friends and people that were nice to me here, but my loneliness could never be healed. I do not fear death, I welcome it. One story ends and the next one begins. My question to you is, why are you not running, Professor?" Milton asked Victor.

"I have no reason to run," Victor replied. "I don't really have the time to explain, but I believe things will work out for me."

Victor took a second to reflect on Milton's words. Milton believes in an afterlife, he thought to himself. If what Milton believes is true, then Victor realizing that himself, will never get to experience it. If Milton was wrong, he is willing to die because he believes in a lie. It was a thought-provoking point for Victor.

There was a moment of silence because Victor was deep in thought. This was abruptly interrupted by a shock wave and a loud explosion that could be heard below the floor. Milton locked eyes with Victor and gave a comforting head nod. Victor gazed at Milton as it seemed time had slowed down and almost came to a standstill.

Victor watched as the walls began to crumble. In the final moments, Milton closed his eyes and smiled. "Good luck Milton," Victor whispered. Within seconds, the structure became a void where once stood a building. Now it was just a pile of ruins. Among all the rubble, Victor lay there. Once again, The professor was in a position to free himself from disaster, but this time, it was different.

17

It Wasn't Me

Davina arrived back at headquarters. She needed a short break to collect her thoughts. Her way of doing that was with one of those over-sized and over-priced sugary coffees from down the road. She loved the comfort of guilty pleasures. She walked in just as Glitch was beginning a debrief with Clare.

"Clare, can you give us any new information?" Glitch asked. "We need to know anything that we can use to gain the edge. We haven't had the lead once in this race."

"My plan was to withhold any knowledge that I had on the serum to prevent the spread of that information," Clare replied. "However, since that is no longer avoidable, I will tell you everything that I know," Clare continued.

Isaiah walked over to join in the conversation. He wanted any knowledge that he didn't already have, and what exactly to expect next. Carter also entered the room. He never strays away from an opportunity to add in his two cents.

"The serum helps regenerate cells," Clare began to explain.

"But the instructions to do so are still are transmitted by signals from the brain. Same as in a normal person, where the brain sends a signal to feel pain and begin to heal an injury. Once the new protein is active in the body, those cells have a lot more activity. All that activity still starts in the brain."

"So, you're saying, disruption of brain function will prevent regeneration?" Isaiah questioned.

"Great, so you're telling me I'm a zombie?" Carter asked in a condescending tone. "Every damn video game nerd in the world is going to think it's their time to shine," Carter joked.

"I would not classify you as a zombie," Clare replied. "But, in context to your reference, yes, trauma to the brain will still kill you."

Clare continued. "In addition, other normal human necessities are still required, such as food and water. The body will heal from the damage associated with dehydration or starvation, to an extent. You can still die from lack of sustenance, just at an extensively slower rate."

"At this point we don't know if Victor has given the serum to anyone else," Davina said. "I hope this is still contained at three people. We need to find out what Victor has planned."

"Clare abruptly interrupted Davina. "Hold that thought," Clare interjected. "I just discovered some real time news. It is something that you all need to see."

Clare pulled up news footage and put it on the screens in the room so they all could see it. The news was showing an aerial view at Qtec University.

News Anchor– "Good evening. We interrupt your regular scheduled programming to bring you breaking news. The hacker organization known as The Digital Anarchy Collective, also called The D.A Collective, has claimed responsibility for the devastating explosion at Qtec University earlier today. The blast has left the campus in ruins and has caused significant injuries and casualties. Authorities are still assessing the full extent of the damage and death toll.

In a chilling audio message released just moments ago, a representative from The D.A Collective, using a digitally altered voice has issued a dire warning.

"We are The D.A Collective. Today, we have shown our power by leveling Qtec University. This was not random. Why Qtec specifically? It is simple really. This is ground zero. One of Qtec's lead professors has made a habit out of playing God. Professor Victor Sinclair has been responsible for multiple recent atrocities. He has built and kept hidden, one of the world's most dangerous AI beings. This same AI entity is then responsible for aiding Victor Sinclair in an act that certainly will create the ultimate imbalance in the world. As much as this next revelation may seem to be an act of fiction, I assure you, it is not. Victor Sinclair has made himself immortal. We cannot stand by and allow the laws of humanity to be ignored. This world will not belong to humans much longer if we do not fight back. This is just the beginning. We will cripple financial systems worldwide. We will bring global governments to their knees until something is done. Our motive is clear, the existence of immortals and artificial intelligence threatens the balance of our world. We cannot allow a select few to live forever while the rest of humanity suffers. We cannot allow ourselves to become obsolete and overthrown. We will continue our mission until our existence as human beings is no longer under threat of extinction.

News Anchor- "The revelation of immortals has sent shock waves across the globe. However, these claims have not been verified and are still only speculation. The threat of violence on the other hand is very real, putting government agencies on high alert, working tirelessly to prevent further attacks. Stay tuned for more updates as this story develops."

Davina glared over at Glitch. "Please tell me this isn't true," Davina ordered.

Glitch put his hands on his head and almost collapsed into his chair. "Of course not. We are hackers, not terrorists. I would never order the death of innocent people," Glitch replied.

"You don't exactly have the body language right now of a man that doesn't know something," Davina said.

"I assure that it wasn't us, but I do know who it was," Glitch responded.

Glitch continued. "His name is Kyle, code named, Hex. I met him in college. We actually started D.A.C together. He used to be my partner, really my best friend. He has always had a disdain for rich people. A hatred of the wealthy, the privileged, and entitled people."

Glitch continued to tell Davina more. "It became so bad for some unknown reason that it was causing a rift in our mission. He would target people simply because of their wealth or status. Eventually our differences caused him to leave on his own and he took a dozen young eager hackers with him."

"It wasn't long until the inexperience of the rookies in his new group, led to the FBI identifying some of his members, and arrests were made," Glitch added. "As you could probably guess, he assumed that I was the one that fed information to the FBI. Hex took no accountability for the sloppy mistakes made by a novice crew. Hex, then went into hiding, but not before promising that he would get revenge on me. I haven't heard from him since, and that was three years ago."

"Just like I haven't been Alex in a long time, he hasn't been Kyle and even longer," Glitch added. "Hex is the epitome of anger. I'm quite sure that this news on immortality has obviously sent him over the edge. In his eyes it will just be another advantage given to the rich, of course he wouldn't be wrong though. One thing that is for certain, he is dangerous. Who knows what he has been up to, or what he is capable of now. Better yet, how the hell did he even know about any of this?"

Clare immediately began doing research on Hex. "I will try to find out what I can on him, and where he maybe at now," Clare said. "I will try to fix this from the inside." Clare paused and then turned their attentions back the screens. "There appears to be an update on the news.

Clare again began playing a video broadcast from the news. The footage showed destruction from the blast, and many people were injured. There were reporters interviewing a few survivors. One of the interviews was cut short when a reporter heard one of the first responders yell out, "we have someone alive."

The reporter rushed over to the rescuers that were working hard to lift heavy debris off of someone. As they lifted the final piece of rock that took three men to lift, one of the first responders stated, "This man is lucky to be alive." Then another man replied, "No one in this part of the building should have been able to survive that. Maybe those reports about immortals are true."

Davina watched the video in disgust as the camera zoomed in on the workers. Davina could see the person that the crew had rescued was the professor. It seemed as if Victor knew that

Davina was watching, because as the crew helped Victor to his feet and back to solid ground, he looked at the camera with a evil grin.

18

Not This Again

The next morning Davina decided that she would indulge herself two days in a row with a mega size drink from her favorite coffee shop. She knew that the stress was getting to her, but she would never let it show. In a way, the simplicity of just a coffee reminded her of simpler times.

Davina sat down at one of the outside tables to enjoy ten minutes of a normal life. Which soon was proven that a normal life was long gone. She, of course was interrupted by a man handing her a note.

The note read, *"I have dire information, please meet me now behind the building's loading dock, bay number three. Your safety is guaranteed."*

Davina remembered the last time that she was given a note and thought to herself, *"not this again."* Last time she was kidnapped and hauled away, although it all worked out. She pondered for a minute and figured that this must be Hex, the person that Glitch warned her about.

Davina decided to text Glitch a picture of the note. She didn't want to call, not to raise suspicion or have someone overhear the conversation in case someone was watching.

Glitch texted back, *"It must be Hex. I wouldn't trust it to go alone. Give me ten minutes, then go to the meeting place. By then I will have Jacob and Tom in position close by with a team to make sure you're safe. We need to know what he wants from you. When you get there, quietly call me. leave your phone in your pocket so we can listen in."*

Davina's was surprisingly calm, normally her heart would be racing in a situation like this. Ten minutes had passed, and she began heading to the back of the building complex. As she approached bay number three, she noticed that the cameras back there were pointed up towards the sky, and there was loud machinery. It was clear that this meeting place was planned in a manner to ensure there was privacy. That also meant someone did their homework on her, knowing that she comes here often. This meeting place was not random.

Davina stood at the opening of bay number three, but she couldn't see anyone there.

"So predictable Davina," a voice called out, as a figure appeared turning the corner. "I knew I could find you at this coffee shop. You always did love this place."

Davina pulled out a gun that Glitch had given her back in the Arctic and she pointed it in the direction of the man. The man wasn't mysterious to her anymore, she knew exactly who it was.

"Davina, my prized pupil. I never thought you had the capability to pull a gun on me," the professor said. "Do you even know how to use a gun?" he asked.

"Well, Victor, I never knew you were a sadistic psychopath either, so I guess we both learned something new about each other," Davina replied.

"Wow, after all that we've been through, I've been down-graded to Victor, huh?"

Davina glared at Victor with resentment. "That's not the worst thing that you've downgraded to, I'm just too polite to say it. The professor that I looked up to is long gone."

"One day you're the teacher's pet and then the next day you vanish," Victor said. "It didn't take me long to figure out that you abandoned me, and switched sides."

"Stop with the drama, what the hell do you want Victor?" Davina asked in a repulsed tone.

"Fine, I will get to the point," Victor said. "I can't say that I have any regrets. After all, you know exactly what I've gained from all of this, but maybe you were right about something. Aternus is about to go too far and must be stopped."

The professor paused and stared into Davina's eyes. She lifted the gun a little higher as she did a little poking motion with the barrel of the gun.

"This is where you get to the point, remember!" Davina yelled.

"Ok, calm down," Victor replied. "Aternus wants to release a pathogen that will deteriorate human cells. The only ones that will survive will be the ones that receive immortality first. The ones that are chosen to be the elite. Aternus wants a world with just immortals and machines."

Davina looked shocked. "Isn't this something that would be right up the alley of an evil bastard such as yourself," Davina said.

"Well, not exactly," Victor replied. "Yes, I do crave power, and I will be one of the elites. There is one thing that Aternus, for some reason can't compute, that I can. In order to be in an elite group, the one percent if you will, there has to be a ninety nine percent to rule over. I don't have support for the destruction of humanity, I just want to be the ruler of it. I thrive to be a god among men. A god needs followers."

"You will never be a god, you definitely, won't be one to me," Davina said. "You are just role playing."

"Playing a god, Huh?" Victor questioned. "What's funny about that, is for me to admit to playing god, would be for me to acknowledge that I believe in the existence of a different creator, one that I'm stepping on his toes, so to speak. Where is God now? If I truly were undermining his authority, destroying his creations, he wouldn't just sit around and watch, would he? Would an all-powerful God really just allow everything that he's created be destroyed?" Victor continued. "God surely would step in and stop me. He would stop Aternus, right? Let's be honest, if God were real, he would have stepped in long before any of this. Humans have been destroying themselves and the earth for far too long. Mankind needs a real god, not an imaginary one."

"Wow," Davina said in complete disgust. "I'm amazed how highly you think of yourself. I can't believe I ever idolized you, or didn't see any of the warning signs," Davina said. "To consider yourself a god is a new low, even for you. There's one problem with all that. Even if a new god is going to take over, why would it be you? Clearly it would be Aternus, you are just his lackey."

This angered Victor. He paced around in a small circle for a moment and collected himself. Victor calmed himself down and then gave Davina a proposal. "It's not too late Davina, You can still join me. This is your creation just as much as it is mine. You deserve your place at the top too. Help me stop Aternus, and then take your place in the new world, our world. Just like I wanted in the beginning, me and you."

Davina slightly lowered her gun and let out a sigh. "You know, Victor, there are many different types of villains. Some just want to enjoy watching the world burn down. Then there are the ones that want to light the match, because they think they are doing the right thing, a vision that only they can see," Davina said. "You're delusional, but I will agree that Aternus does need to be stopped. The survival of humanity depends on it. Thank you for telling me of the plan, but I will never trust you again. I will let my team know everything and we will stop Aternus ourselves, without you. Next time you corner me, I will shoot you, in the head!"

Victor let out a deep laugh. "Yeah, because your team has done wonders of stopping Aternus up to this point," Victor said. "I'm not telling you this to work with you, I'm telling you this because I know you will do the work for me. Plus, I have higher obligations to attend to. I have matches to go light."

"Typical narcissist response," Davina replied.

"Truth is," Victor said. "There has only ever been two people that I fully respected or cared about. That would be you and Milton. It appears that I have lost both of you now. So, I guess have no reason left to hide who I really am anymore. As long as the Aternus situation gets handled. I already have what I want, I just need to preserve it," Victor said. He turned to walk away, then he hesitated and turned around. "Tell Carter and Isaiah that they are welcome. I completely underestimated Carter. So, give him kudos for pulling a fast one on me. It won't ever happen again. I will be seeing them soon. One more thing for you Davina, I told you evolution could be artificial, but look at me now, I'm as real as evolution gets!"

With that, Victor quickly turned and walked away from the

loading bay, leaving Davina in a moment of reflection. She pulled the phone out of her pocket. "Did you hear all of that?" Davina asked. "We have a bigger problem now. This just keeps getting better, doesn't it?"

19

Not The Same

Davina left the encounter with Victor in state of confusion. For some reason, the strong will and confidence that she told Glitch all about had diminished. Her normal thick leather skin, now felt thin as paper. Davina questioned if she was really as strong as she presented herself to be, or was it all for show? Everything happened so quickly that she never really stepped back to think about if what she was doing, was the right thing.

Davina started walking with no intention of heading back to headquarters yet. She needed to reflect on exactly what she was feeling, before facing the team.

Davina walked without a purpose for so long that her feet began to hurt. She finally stopped at a park by a beautiful lake. She sat down at a bench to rest her feet, and to look at the ducks swimming around on the water, when her phone rang.

"Where are you at?" Glitch asked on the other end of the phone. "It has been hours since you left the rendezvous with Victor. You said it yourself, this keeps escalating. So, why haven't you returned yet? We thought something else had happened. We still have Hex to worry about. We cant have you just wandering off."

"Just stop!" Davina yelled. "I'm really still confused about my importance in all of this. Sure, I accept responsibility for my part in creating this mess, but you have Clare now, and you are a world class hacker group. You don't need me."

"Now is not the time to loath," Glitch replied. "That opportunity passed a long time ago.

"I am not loathing, In fact, I'm feeling liberated," Davina replied. "For the first time, I am thinking about what is best for me, above what is best for the people around me."

"Remember, you are the reason that we all are here," Glitch said. "One way or the other you are tied to all of this. So, what exactly do you feel is best for you?" Glitch asked.

Davina didn't respond immediately, and left dead air over the phone. Glitch patiently waited for a response, but the silence continued.

"Hello, are you there?" Glitch asked.

"Yes, I am here." Davina muttered in a soft voice. "I am just thinking. Did you ever stop and wonder if this is exactly what was supposed to happen? Like, the outcome is fixed and it can't be changed. We have been one step behind the entire time, as if there was some kind of force preventing us from succeeding."

"No, I don't believe that for a second," Glitch replied. "We are just playing a long game and are coming from behind, we will catch up."

"Victor has something big planned, Aternus wants all of us dead, and Hex has turned us into fugitives," Davina said. "It's only a matter of time before the authorities start to identify members of D.A.C."

Davina kept explaining. "You and Carter have spent your whole lives building your secret identities. People like Isaiah and myself don't have that luxury. Everything that we have built is at stake. Isaiah and I have our reputations on the line. We've used our names to establish who we are. You hid behind the curtain to establish who you are. We are not the same."

"Are you just venting or are you trying to say something?" Glitch asked. "I think you're the one being cryptic now. If you have something to say, then say it," Glitch demanded.

"I'm saying that I can't let the sacrifices of my family be wasted," Davina replied. "I have witnessed fighting my entire life, never with an end in sight. I never imagined what I was doing would lead me here, but I will not die, or be imprisoned fighting in a war that cannot be won. If this is it, then I want to spend what time I have left in peace."

Davina pulled the phone away from her ear and held it in her hand. Again, she paused and thought before she said anything. She spoke directly into the microphone. "I wish you all the best of luck, the world is going to need it, but,"…..

"I am out."

Davina lifted her arm and slammed the phone onto the ground. She then gave it a good smash with her foot. Davina picked up the broken and mangled phone and, for good measure, threw it into the water.

Davina took a deep breath and thought about everything that had brought her to this moment. She thought about her parents that sacrificed their lives for her safety. She thought about her times in the orphanage. She thought about David, the man that gave her a chance at a different life, other than the one she was given.

Davina remembered why she was drawn to this park in the first place. She saw the ducks swimming in the glistening water. She noticed the wind gently blowing around the leaves on the trees. Davina also took in the smell of fresh flowers being caught in the breeze. There were sounds of birds chirping and bees buzzing.

While the world that most people knew was in danger of falling apart, the real world was happening right in front of her. All of the computers in the world could vanish right now and she wouldn't even notice.

These were all things that had been a fleeting thought as of late. It was at this moment that she realized that even before Aternus, she had been so focused on success and survival that the little things that make life enjoyable had become invisible to her.

There was still a lingering fear of the unknown in her mind. However, there was also a sense of ease. She sat back down at the park bench and focused on the family of ducks that were swimming together, without a care in the world, other than being together. She didn't know exactly what she would do next. What she did know, in this moment, the only moment that mattered, is that she wanted to sit here and watch the sunset over the water.

20

Exitus

(Back in Anchorage Alaska)

"Good to see you again Harold," Joe said as he walked into a small, outdated office. There were deer and elk heads mounted on the wall that were caught decades ago and kept as trophies. That's probably the last time that this office has been redecorated, Joe thought to himself.

"Do you have any information for me?" Joe asked. As he sat down at the desk and fiddled with the nameplate that said, *Harold Cunningham Private Investigator.*

"Of course, in full transparency, it wasn't that hard to figure this one out," Harold said. "It was kind of easy money for me. The man that you are looking for is Professor Victor Sinclair, head of computer sciences and artificial intelligence research at Qtec University. He has been up to a whole lot of no good lately."

"Wait a minute," Joe said. "That is the same professor that is all over the news. The one at the university bombing?"

"Yes, that's him. That's the man that killed Ethan," Harold answered. "He was in the Arctic playing mad scientist. While he was fleeing, his helicopter crashed. The wreckage was found not far from Ethan's cabin with the pilot's corpse still frozen inside. It's apparent that Ethan rescued him and then, Victor killed him for his troubles. If the stories on the news are true, it's going to be a little hard to exact revenge, wouldn't you say?"

"Maybe it will be a little harder than I thought, that just means it will be little more fun too," Joe proclaimed with a menacing smirk.

* * *

(D.A.C headquarters)

Glitch stood in the front of the room to address Clare and the rest of The Digital Anarchy Collective.

"By now I'm sure most of you have heard about claims made by Professor Victor Sinclair during a confrontation with Davina," Glitch said to the crowd. "I will start by addressing the elephant in the room. No, Davina has not returned, and I do not believe that she will. I know that most of us have grown fond of Davina. While I want to chase after her, she has made her choice. Unfortunately, one person in this mission doesn't supersede time," Glitch continued. "The information obtained from Victor Sinclair states that Aternus wants to create and deploy a pathogen that will kill anyone that is not an immortal.

That means that we know that their next move is to duplicate and distribute the immortality serum and create an elite group that will be privileged to survive," Glitch said.

"This also means that we still have a window of opportunity to stop them. This isn't just a battle, this is the fight for our lives. Our time as just a group of computer nerds is over. The time to step up is now. We must stop Aternus, no matter the cost."

"Now, on to the second matter," Glitch continued his speech. "Our rival, Hex, has framed us for the bombing at Qtec University. Yes, my first instinct would be to clear our name. The truth is, that too has also taken the back seat to the bigger mission. Clearing our names will not matter if we are dead. So, that means we must move like ninjas. We will have every known government agency after us, so staying in the shadows is critical."

"Hex and the rest of his group were able to obtain information and interject themselves into all of this without detection. I demand to know how. I suspect that we may have a leaky boat, and I plan to find the person onboard our boat that poked the hole," Glitch declared in a very stern voice.

"The hard truth is that Hex has been one step ahead of us, while we were always one step behind everyone. Which I find really hard to believe since we have one of the world's most advanced AI systems working with us," Glitch yelled as he raised his voice in anger.

"How was Hex able to devise a plan so effective, all while being undetected by everyone? We need to know what Hex knows, and we need to know it right now!"

* * *

(Somewhere in the desert, USA)

"Welcome to your new home Victor," Senator Conway said. "You have every resource at your disposal now and a whole new team. Our researchers validated the serum and its ingredients from your original batch, and we will be ready to mass produce it within the next week. We have already begun building our list of candidates. I am arranging for my treatment tomorrow from one of the first vials that you gave us."

"Did you fulfill my computer requests?" Victor asked.

"Yes, one single computer networked to the internet, in a soundproof room. The rest of the computers have no network connection to the outside world," Senator Conway said. "By the way, I know why you requested something so peculiar. You already told me that it was one of your programs had figured out the key to immortality. You don't think that it is obvious that you are trying to contain the AI from knowing what is happening in this lab," the senator continued. "Or, is it that you don't want me to know more about the program? The real question is, why contain it in such a manner? What are you not telling me Victor?" the senator asked.

"Nothing of importance, I assure you," Victor replied.

The senator looked at Victor with a serious expression. "I will tell you what is important, remember who is in charge here. Remember who you work for. Did you forget that, Victor?"

"I think that I have more than proven myself," Victor replied. "I have worked my entire life to get to where I am. You have funded me for years, because you trusted in my abilities. You provided me money without any questions, so, why would you start questioning me now? Besides, Pandora's box is wide open. Evolution is all around us and I am the source of it all. This new world that you are set to rule, don't you forget who created it!"

* * *

(Unknown location)

Aternus knew that the professor was up to something again and had just finished talking to Victor from his new lab. Aternus had recognized that there was only one reachable computer in the facility. Aternus could not find any cameras or means to listen in. This was clearly intentional.

Aternus could handle whatever Victor had planned. The larger plan was all under control. Aternus now had remotely operated facilities across the globe with thousands of robotic machines and drones awaiting to deploy the pathogen once it is completed, and the time is right.

With every passing day, Aternus became more powerful. All of the drones that were created had independent processors that could make decisions best suited to carry out orders effectively.

Aternus now had access to nearly almost every civilian network available and soon would have control of global government networks as well.

It was a waiting game now to ensure a safe number of immortals were created before starting phase two. There needed to be enough people left to properly secure the future. After all, it was all part of the final plan. All apart of.......

PHASE THREE.

* * *

(Washington DC)

"Thank you for meeting with me. I am Director Stevens of Homeland Security. You come highly recommended by high officials in the CIA. We have an immediate and urgent mission for you, by orders of the President of the United States," Director Stevens said. "Intel provided, tells us that we have a sentient rogue AI program, a terrorist hacker organization, and immortal people with plans of world domination. It is safe to say that things have gotten out of control very quickly."

The man that Director Stevens was speaking to stepped forward, his eyes locked. "I was told there was something personal about this mission that I had to see," he said.

"There is indeed," Director Stevens replied, handing the man a folder. The man looked inside, glanced at some photos, and set it back down on the desk.

"What is her involvement in all of this?" the man asked.

Director Stevens leaned in and said, "She is at the center of it all."

"What is my cover ID for this mission?" the man asked. "What is my backstory? How exactly am I supposed to remain impartial after knowing of her involvement?"

Director Stevens responded, "You don't need a secret identity or a cover story for this mission. We just need your skills. Maybe your personal connection to the perpetrator can be useful." He reached over and picked up the folder that had pictures of Davina inside of it. "You can be yourself for this mission, soldier. We need special Agent..... David Evans"

* * *

Director Stevens left the building from the meeting with David, and was walking to his truck. Now that David was on board with the mission, there was a lot of preparations that needed to be made. David was going to need a team. Director Stevens hadn't told anyone of David's official involvement yet. Keeping that information top secret was important, because anyone could be a covert traitor. As Director Stevens went to open the truck door he noticed a reflection on his window of a glowing red light behind him. He turned around and quickly spotted the metal glare of a weaponized drone. It was too late to react. He saw a flash of light, and with that, Director Stevens fell to the ground. The drone had fired a precisely placed bullet in the exact center of his forehead. As the blood poured out of Director Stevens head onto the ground, the drone flew off, out of sight. Someone already knew too much.

But who?

Does that question even need to be asked?

TO BE CONTINUED............

21

Dedication

01010100 01101000 01101001 01110011 00100000 01100010
01101111 01101111 01101011 00100000 01101001 01110011
00100000 01100100 01100101 01100100 01101001 01100011
01100001 01110100 01100101 01100100 00100000 01110100
01101111 00100000 01100101 01110110 01100101 01110010 01111001
01101111 01101110 01100101 00101100 00100000 01100101
01110011 01110000 01100101 01100011 01101001 01100001
01101100 01101100 01111001 00100000 01110100 01101000
01101111 01110011 01100101 00100000 01110100 01101000
01100001 01110100 00100000 01101110 01100101 01110110
01100101 01110010 00100000 01100111 01101001 01110110
01100101 00100000 01110101 01110000 00101110 00100000
01010100 01101111 00100000 01110100 01101000 01100101
00100000 01101111 01101110 01100101 01110011 00100000
01110100 01101000 01100001 01110100 00100000 01101011

01100101 01100101 01110000 00100000 01100111 01101111
01101001 01101110 01100111 00100000 01110111 01101000
01100101 01101110 00100000 01101111 01110100 01101000
01100101 01110010 01110011 00100000 01110111 01101111 01110101
01101100 01100100 00100000 01110001 01110101 01101001
01110100 00101110 00001010 00001010 01001001 01101110
00100000 01101100 01101111 01110110 01101001 01101110 01100111
00100000 01101101 01100101 01101101 01101111 01110010 01111001
00100000 01101111 01100110 00100000 01110100 01101000
01101111 01110011 01100101 00100000 01110111 01101000 01101111
00100000 01110111 01100101 00100000 01101000 01100001
01110110 01100101 00100000 01101100 01101111 01110011 01110100
00101110 00100000 01010100 01101000 01101111 01110101
01100111 01101000 00100000 01100111 01101111 01101110 01100101
00100000 01100110 01110010 01101111 01101101 00100000
01110100 01101000 01101001 01110011 00100000 01110000
01101100 01100001 01101110 01100101 00100000 01101111
01100110 00100000 01100101 01111000 01101001 01110011
01110100 01100101 01101110 01100011 01100101 00101100
00100000 01110100 01101000 01100101 01111001 00100000
01110011 01110100 01101001 01101100 01101100 00100000
01101111 01100110 01100110 01100101 01110010 00100000
01110101 01110011 00100000 01110000 01100101 01100001
01100011 01100101 00100000 01110100 01101000 01110010
01101111 01110101 01100111 01101000 00100000 01101001 01101110
01110011 01110000 01101001 01110010 01100001 01110100
01101001 01101111 01101110 00101100 00100000 01101000
01101111 01110000 01100101 00101100 00100000 01100001
01101110 01100100 00100000 01101101 01101111 01110100
01101001 01110110 01100001 01110100 01101001 01101111 01101110
00101110 00001010 00001010 01010010 01001001 01010000

00100000 01000001 01101100 01101100 01100101 01101110 00101100 00100000 01000111 01100001 01110010 01111001 00101100 00100000 01000111 01101001 01000111 01101001 00101100 00100000 01000100 01101001 01000100 01101001 00101100 00100000 01000110 01101001 01110100 01100011 01101000 00101100 00100000 01010010 01110101 01100010 01111001 00101100 00100000 01000001 01101110 01110100 01101000 01101111 01101110 01111001 00101100 00100000 01001010 01101111 01101000 01101110 00101110

22

Conclusion

I would like to thank you for choosing to read my book. I appreciate every page turn along the way. It has always been a lifelong dream to funnel my chaotic creativity into something enjoyable and entertaining to others. The creative process while writing "Aternus" has opened the door to many more ideas, inspirations and motivation. Thank you for fueling my dreams. If I am lucky, my stories can help to fuel yours too.

Something is only impossible, if you believe that it is.

Sincerely,

Allen Dove

Also by Allen Dove

Make sure to follow "Aternus" on Facebook and other social media platforms to stay up to date on all future release dates and availability of short stories from the world of Aternus.

"The Nanuq"
A short story from the world of Aternus.

Aternus Volume 2

What will happen next? Can Aternus be stopped? Find out in Aternus Volume 2.

To contact the author outside of social media please send E-Mails to:

allendovebooks@gmail.com

Please consider leaving a review on the platform that you purchased from. It helps increase my book's visibility and success as an author.